Stolen Moments

STOLEN MOMENTS BOOK I

CATHARINA MAURA

Dedication

For my husband, who is my biggest fan and my greatest support. I couldn't have done this without you.

Thank you for believing in me when I fail to believe in myself. So many of my dreams wouldn't have come true without you.

Chapter One

EMILIA

"Don't look now, but he's staring at you again," Kate whispers. I blush and try to glance at Zach as discreetly as I can. I totally fail, of course. I'm anything but subtle. He catches me staring at him from across the cafeteria and grins as he throws a wink my way. My cheeks heat and I turn back around so quickly that I nearly fall out of my chair. Kate looks at me in disbelief. "I said *don't look*!" she whisper-shouts. I bury my face in my hands to hide my embarrassment and Kate gasps. "Oh, my god. *Oh my god*, Milly. He's coming this way. He's walking right towards us."

I peek at her through my fingers to make sure she isn't joking. Her shocked expression tells me she isn't messing with me, and I suddenly forget how to act like an actual human being. Zach is one of the hottest guys in school and I've had a crush on him for as long as I can remember. He's in Carter's grade, so he's two years older than Kate and me. For him to even speak to me makes my heart race. Our town is tiny and almost everyone knows each other, but it's still not that common for a senior to speak to a sophomore like me. And... it's *Zach*.

1

"Hey, Emilia," he says, dropping into the seat next to mine. Oh my god. Zach is actually sitting next to me. He puts his arm on the back of my seat and I nearly stop functioning. "Haven't seen you around for a while," he murmurs.

Instead of replying I just stare at him, beyond flustered. "I... I... I had the flu," I stammer.

Zach smiles at me, and my heart does a somersault. "Hope you're all better now, babe."

I nod and stare at him, still in disbelief that he's actually sitting here speaking to me. And did he just call me babe? I practically swoon. I glance around us to find some of the girls in my grade looking at me with blatant jealousy. Zach is widely considered to be the second hottest guy in school. The top spot is reserved for asshole Carter. I don't see the appeal. It's obvious the girls in my school are delusional. I guess he does have gorgeous hazel eyes that look a little green in certain lighting, and his thick dark hair is pretty nice. He's also super tall and keeps getting more and more muscular, but whatever. It's Carter. His rotten personality definitely overshadows his slightly good looks.

"Yeah, all good now," I reply, finally snapping out of it. Zach is *talking* to me. There's no way I'll ruin this opportunity, nerves be damned.

"That's good," he murmurs. "because I was kinda wondering what you're doing on Saturday. I'm having a few people over at my house. Thought you might wanna hang out?"

I blink, my mind completely blank. Did he just... Is he asking me out? I guess not, because he said there'd be more people. But *still*, it's more than I ever expected. I blush and Zach smiles smugly. He leans in as though he's about to brush my hair out of my face, but before his fingers make contact with my hair, a hand closes around his wrist. I look up to find Carter staring down at me.

"Goddamn it," I mutter under my breath. Carter's sole mission in life seems to be to annoy me. We've been feuding with each other since the day we met, and over the years our war has only intensified. I've tried my best to keep my teeny tiny crush on Zach from Carter, because that type of knowledge would be weaponized in his hands. He grits his teeth and looks away from me, focusing on Zach instead. Zach's shoulders sink and he purses his lips, clearly disappointed that Carter interrupted us.

"What do you want?" I snap.

He ignores me and stares Zach down. "Kate and Emilia aren't allowed to go to parties until they're sixteen," he says, grinning evilly. "So please tell me you weren't just inviting them to this weekend's house party?"

He pushes Zach's wrist away and stands in between us. I'm tempted to poke him where I know he's ticklish, but I don't want to come across as childish or petty in front of Zach.

"Ah, I didn't know, dude," Zach says. My heart sinks. He's going to take back his invite, all because of Carter.

"That's odd, because I vaguely recall mentioning it to you when you asked me about Emilia yesterday," Carter says. Zach cups the back of his neck and looks down. Not only are Carter and Zach in the same grade, they're also on the football team together. There's no way he'd choose me over Carter. I'm never getting an invite now.

"It's fine. I mean, you don't live that far. I could drop by," I say, trying to sound as upbeat as I can.

Carter laughs humorlessly and turns to look at me. "Like hell you will," he says. He glares at me and I glare right back at him.

Zach stands up and looks at Carter, ignoring me entirely. "Look, I hear you. No hard feelings, man," he says.

I stand up too, but Zach shakes his head. He winks at me and then walks away. I bite my lip to keep from murdering Carter in cold blood.

"You — you... you're such a dick!" I shout. I push against his chest, but I fail to move him. In the last year he's gone from thin and my height to muscular and tall. I hate it. I hate that I now have to raise my head to look into his eyes. I push against him harder and he grabs my hands, keeping them in place.

3

"If I catch you trying to go to any parties before you're sixteen, I'll tell your dad," he says.

I huff and roll my eyes. Like my dad would actually care. With each year that passes by, he works more hours and spends less time with me. He's become a shell of the person he used to be. Every once in a while he'll make a remark that tells me he's just reminded of my mom whenever he looks at me. I can't even remember the last time we had dinner together. He's definitely not going to care if I go to a party.

"I'll tell my mom too," Carter says.

That asshole. He knows Helen is my weakness. The idea of her being disappointed in me breaks my heart, and he knows it. He grins like he knows he's got me now and lets go of my hands. His eyes move to Kate and he stares at her with raised brows.

"*What?*" she says. "I didn't do anything. Go tell mom all you want."

I chuckle when Carter glares at her before storming off. I inhale deeply and sit down in my seat. I push my tray of half eaten food away, my appetite long gone.

Kate huffs and stares at Carter's disappearing form. Her stunning eyes are identical to Carter's and they're flashing with anger. "I can't believe he just cock blocked you like that. I mean... I know you two have your feud and all that, but damn. This is next level."

I look up at her, suddenly realizing that she's right. "He did, didn't he?" I snap.

Kate nods, furious on my behalf. She crosses her arms and bites her lip. "Maybe we can sneak into the party," she murmurs. "How cool would it be if we actually went? I know Zach hasn't invited anyone else in our grade, he never does. This would've been a first. Damn Carter. I can't believe he ruined this for us."

I laugh. "I can't believe that's what you're concerned about. Kate, he ruined my chances with Zach! Didn't you see the way Zach looked at me before he walked away from us? I know that look. It's the same way Tommy looked when Carter told him to stay away from me last year. I can't believe he did that to me when he goes around sleeping with half the school. Don't even pretend it isn't true."

Kate looks disgusted at the idea of her brother sleeping around. She flicks her long auburn hair over her shoulder and sighs. He's a total dick to me, but he treats his mother and his sister like they're the most precious people alive. He's always polite and caring to them, while he saves his crudeness and malice for me.

"I'm sure that's not true," she says, looking away. The mere idea of Carter sleeping around makes her uncomfortable, but she and I both know that it *is* true. She's heard the same rumors that I have. She just chooses to believe that they're merely that. *Rumors.*

"Ugh," I groan. I bury my hands in my hair and seethe in silence. "I'm going to get him for this."

Kate nods in agreement. Usually she tries to dissuade me from arguing with Carter, but today she's on my side.

"What're you gonna do?" she asks with a hint of excitement. I grin and wink at her, leaving her to wonder what I'm planning.

Chapter Two

EMILIA

I walk into Kate's house as if it were my own, like I've done almost every day since I moved here seven years ago. Helen looks up at me and smiles.

"How was school, sweetie?" she asks, like she does every single day. Helen has shown me what it's like to have a real mother. From the start she's treated me exactly the same way that she treats Kate, and over the years I've come to love her just as much as I love Kate. Helen is one of my favorite people in the world.

Years ago my dad asked her to watch me after school while he was at work, and the habits we developed then have remained. Even now, I'm usually at the Clarke's house after school. I'll go home to change and to drop my bag, and then I'll go straight next door. More often than not I'll have dinner here before going back when my dad finally gets home. It seems like he works more overtime every year, and I can't help but wonder if it might be because he doesn't want to spend time with me. When he comes home, he usually goes straight to bed. He barely even looks at me.

"School was good. I aced my math test," I tell Helen. She gasps and smiles from ear to ear.

Carter rolls his eyes and coughs as he shouts, "Nerd!"

I glare at him and look away, intent on ignoring him. I'm not over that stunt he pulled with Zach a few days ago. Besides, he's one to talk. Carter is one of those horrible people that are good at everything they do. His grades are top-notch and he's the school's quarterback too. I hate him. If only people at school could see past the stupid facade and that stupid smile of his. I'm the only one that sees the devil within. Even Helen and Kate adore him.

"Oh, honey. I'm so proud of you," Helen says. She walks to the freezer and takes out a tub of my favorite Ben & Jerry's ice cream. My mouth waters just looking at the tub of Chocolate Fudge Brownie.

"For you," she says, pushing it towards me. I grin and reach out to grab it, but Carter gets to it first. He takes the lid off and looks right into my eyes. He grins and then slowly licks the entire top layer.

"Ugh! You're not twelve anymore. Why are you so freaking childish?" I shout.

I lunge towards him and he jumps up, out of the way. He holds the ice cream right above my head and I jump up in an attempt to reach it. He's so much taller than me now. I hate it.

"You asshole!" I shout.

Helen clears her throat and looks at us in amusement. "Language, Emilia," she murmurs. None of Carter and my antics have ever fazed her. If anything, she seems to enjoy them. She rarely interferes with our ongoing feud, no matter how bad it gets. I glare at Carter, blaming him for getting chastised.

"You... you... snickerdoodle!"

He bursts out laughing, and I take that moment to aim. I jam my knee up in an attempt to knee him in the balls, but he's become a pro at evading me. He grabs my leg and pulls on it, making me lose my balance. I fall down onto my butt and he

7

laughs before dragging his tongue over my ice cream. That disgusting devil.

Kate walks down the stairs and smiles when she finds me sprawled on the floor. "Thought I heard you," she says. She drops down on the floor beside me, completely ignoring the fact that I'm obviously not sitting here voluntarily.

Carter grabs a spoon and starts eating my ice cream from the tub, his eyes on me with every bite. I'm seething.

"Are you prepared for the mid-year cheering auditions?" Kate asks. I bite down on my lip and shake my head. Kate joined at the start of the year and she's been trying to get me to join her ever since, but I'm just not sure I'm cheerleader material. I'm far better at studying than I am at jumping and dancing. I didn't think Kate would enjoy it either, especially because she's always hated cheerleaders. I guess that changed when the most popular one of them befriended her. Ever since Kate became friends with Gabby, she's started to change, and I'm not a hundred percent sure I like it.

Carter bursts out laughing. "*She's* joining the cheering squad? When hell freezes over, maybe. She'll break a leg in the first week."

I cross my arms over my chest and glare up at him. Carter smiles and takes another bite of my ice cream.

"Yes," I blurt. "I'm ready. I might as well give it a try."

I know deep down I'm only doing it to prove Carter wrong and that I should be above that, but he brings out the worst in me.

Kate grabs my hands excitedly and grins. "Oh my god, really?" she says. My smile wavers. I can't get out of this without letting her down now. Kate looks beyond happy, while Carter looks annoyed. I'm not surprised. I've heard the rumors about him and the girls in the cheering squad. He's probably worried I'll cock block him the way he did to me last week, and I probably will. He deserves it.

Kate pulls me up. She drags me to the staircase and I look back at Carter. He's staring at me, obviously brooding. His eyes meet mine and for a second I see a glimpse of concern. Surely he isn't worried that I'll get injured? I'm a little accident prone, but how hard can cheerleading be?

Kate drags me up the stairs and into her room. "The cheering thing just reminded me I totally forgot to tell you," she says. "Look what I bought my mom for Mother's Day!"

I don't follow and fail to understand what cheering has to do with Helen's Mother's Day present. Kate walks towards her wardrobe and takes out a gorgeous dark blue gown that Helen is definitely going to love. I stare at it, equal parts confused and equal parts stunned. The gown is amazing, but Kate and I have been buying one joint present for Helen for the last three years. Why would she buy something without me?

Each year, Kate and I compete with Carter to give Helen the best Mother's Day gift. Though she refuses to pick one over the other, we both know that we lose more often than we'd like to admit. The devil can be quite thoughtful sometimes — so thoughtful, that Kate and I have had to join hands to surpass him. I stare at the shimmering blue fabric in awe. I guess Kate is definitely winning this year.

"I went to the shopping center with Gabby yesterday, and she recommended this dress for my mom. She has such amazing taste." My heart sinks. Gabby again. She moved here from New York right before the start of the school year and quickly became the most popular girl in our grade — scratch that, in our entire school. She took a liking to Kate almost instantly, and they've been friends ever since. It's because of Gabby that Kate insisted on joining the cheering squad, even though she's always been incredibly introverted. I guess I'm just not used to sharing Kate, and Gabby doesn't really seem to like me much, so they never include me when they hang out.

"I didn't realize we were doing separate gifts this year," I say. Kate's expression drops and I immediately feel bad for bringing it up at all. Kate shouldn't have to discuss anything with me before buying a present, yet I still feel left out. I don't mind it as much when she hangs out with Gabby and doesn't invite me, but this is different. Besides, we still have a couple of months left until Mother's Day. I thought we'd plan something out together. Usually it takes us weeks to even decide.

"Oh, well… I saw this and I thought it would be perfect for my mom. I guess we can give it together? Or maybe you can buy her something else," she says. I hate that I've taken away her excitement over the gown and shake my head, trying my best to shrug it off.

"I should buy Helen matching shoes," I say.

Kate looks at the dress and purses her lips. She's quiet for a couple of moments and then looks up at me with an expression I can't quite decipher. "Well, you know, my mom isn't your mother. You don't need to get her anything at all," she says, her eyes flashing.

I freeze, a pang of hurt coursing through me. Recently she's been making remarks such as this more and more often, and I never know how to respond. I'm always worried about overstepping, and recently she's been making me feel like I am.

"Anyway, we can go to the shopping center tomorrow if you still wanna get something. She's going to absolutely love this gown!"

Kate puts the dress away carefully and sits down on the bed next to me. I'm a little thrown. Recently, I've started to feel like the way Kate treats me has changed. She's always been my best friend — the girl that stuck with me when I was the new girl in a close-knit town. She defended me when kids made fun of me for not having a mother, and she's always done her best to include me in her family, so I'm not sure what I've done to cause the recent change in her.

"So, I saw Carter ate your ice cream," she says. "Mom picked that up especially for you when she bought me some Cookie Dough. It's so sweet of my mom to get you something too, isn't it? You know Carter doesn't even like chocolate. I can't believe he's acting like this after ruining your chances with Zach. I saw the photos from the party, and we really missed out."

I'm enraged instantly. "I know. That dick," I snap. Kate grins and I'm relieved. I hate it when Kate and I are even remotely at odds with each other.

"What're you gonna do?" she asks, giggling. She always tries to dissuade me from arguing with Carter in an attempt to be a good sister, but I know she secretly enjoys our feud.

I glance at her bathroom door and grin. "I have an idea." I walk into her bathroom and emerge with a tube of Nair hair removal cream.

Kate's smile drops, and she looks at me with wide eyes. "Oh my god, Milly. Carter will actually kill you this time."

I shrug and walk out of her room, Kate hot on my heels. As always, she keeps an eye out while I sneak into Carter's room. I giggle and walk into his bathroom, my heart racing. I grab his bottle of shampoo and shake it, happy to find it half empty. I fill it up with Nair and shake vigorously, without an ounce of remorse. Just in the last week, he's thrown itching powder all over my bed, ruined my chances with Zach and eaten my damn ice cream. I can't wait to see his face after his next shower. Maybe this'll finally teach him.

Chapter Three

CARTER

I pause on the stairs when I hear Kate's bedroom door open. Emilia walks out looking like she's on a mission and Kate follows her with a worried expression. I grin when I see the bottle of Nair in her hands. She's getting cleverer and more ruthless. The stakes in our game keep getting higher. Very well, I've gotta hand it to her. This is a good one. I bet she's still mad as hell that I stopped Zach from flirting with her last week. She's been trying to ignore me all week now — I wonder how long it'll take her to get over it. She's too young to be going to parties like Zach's and it's obvious what he wanted from her. No way was I gonna let that happen on my watch. I might mess with her, but when it comes down to it, I'll always protect her the way I protect Kate.

I should've tried to appease her this week and I definitely should've been nicer to her when she got home today instead of eating her ice cream, but I couldn't help myself. That flustered and angry look on her face just makes my day.

Kate is meant to stand watch in front of my room, but all she does is stare at her phone. I could walk right up to her and she wouldn't even notice.

Eventually Emilia emerges from my room with a triumphant look on her face. She looks so damn pleased with herself. She's smiling, and her stunning blue eyes are twinkling with mischief.

I grin to myself and take a few steps back before walking up the stairs, making as much noise as I can. Both of them gasp and hurry back into Kate's room, the door closing just as I make it to the top.

I smile and walk into my room. The perfume I gave Emilia for her last birthday is all over my room, betraying her presence. She claimed she hated the smell, but she wears it every day. I chuckle to myself and shake my head. How she thinks she gets away with these things is beyond me. There are always traces of her.

I strip and walk into my bathroom, scanning the bottles in the shower. She's done a meticulous job. Not a single thing is out of place. I stand underneath the stream for a few minutes and lean back against the wall. What expression will she have on her face if I walk out of here with clumps of my hair missing? I'm filled with excitement and anticipation. She's vicious, that's for sure.

I smile and grab the shampoo bottle, lathering my hair with the Nair-laced concoction. I leave it in for a couple of minutes for good measure. I'm not surprised when chunks of my hair fall out when I rinse the shampoo off. I bite back a smile and shake my head. She really did it, huh?

I turn the shower off and step out to get dressed. I take one look in the mirror and burst out laughing. I look fucking ridiculous. I throw on some shorts and a tee before storming down, my angry game face on. I've learned to school my amused expressions for our feud long ago. I hear the front door slam closed just as I reach the bottom of the stairs and bite back a grin. Dad just got home. Perfect.

I storm into the living room, and my parents look at me with wide eyes when I enter. My hair wasn't very long to begin with, but now there are huge chunks just straight up missing. Everyone's eyes move to Emilia. No one feels the need to point out the obvious. We all know she's the culprit. I wonder if Mom will finally let her have it this time. If I did this to Emilia, I'd be grounded for the rest of my damn life.

Emilia looks at me, but instead of the satisfaction and victory I expected to see, her eyes are filled with horror and remorse. It's not a look I like on her. Through all the shit we've pulled on each other, she's never once looked remorseful, and I've never wanted her to.

My dad clears his throat. "That's something, huh? How did that even happen?" he asks. Kate and I both inherited my dad's eyes — the same eyes that are currently sparkling with amusement when he should be outraged on my behalf. Dad rubs his neck and tries to look stern, but I can see him trying to suppress a smile. Trust him to find this shit funny.

My mother looks at Dad through narrowed eyes. "William," she says, her tone disapproving. Dad shrugs. It's obvious he finds this funny as hell, and I don't think Mom appreciates how hard he finds it to hide his glee.

Mom ignores Dad and instead looks at Emilia with disapproval, and though I've achieved what I wanted to, I find that I don't feel pleased at all. "Emilia, sweetie... What did you do?" my mother asks, her voice stern. Emilia looks up at her and I see the panic building in her eyes. I can tell my mother's disappointment hits her hard and I hate it. She trembles as her eyes fill with tears, and my heart starts to ache at the sight of her.

"You," I say, interrupting the scolding my mother is about to give her. "Come here."

Emilia jumps out of her seat and takes a step back, but I keep stalking towards her. "Shit. I'm sorry, Carter!" she yells.

I shake my head and point at my hair. "I'll make you pay for this."

She dashes into the hallway in an attempt to escape to her own house, but I won't let her. I chase her and she looks at me with wide eyes as she tries to evade me. I chuckle as I lift her into my arms and right over my shoulder. She squeals and fights me, but I hold her down and turn back towards the stairs.

I carry her up the stairs with ease. I'm tempted to slap her ass for thrashing so wildly, but I know she'll kill me if I so much as try. I walk into my bedroom and throw her onto my bed. She sits up, undoubtedly ready to argue with me, but I lift my arms and pull my shirt up and over my head. Emilia freezes and falls silent, her eyes glued to my abs, courtesy of hours and hours of football practice. She blinks as though she's startled, and I grin when she fails to snap out of it. If I'd known that all it takes to get her to shut up was walking around half naked, I'd have started doing it ages ago.

"You're gonna fix this," I say, pointing to my hair. I walk into my bathroom and walk back out with an electric shaver. She takes it with trembling hands and I take hold of her chin, pinching it slightly.

"Mess around with me and it's your hair that's next. You'd better fix this, Minx," I say, addressing her by the nickname I gave her years ago, back when I first learned the definition of the word in English class. She used to hate it, and in retaliation she started to call me Devil — the worst thing she could think of at the time. Little does she know that I hardly find it an insult.

Emilia glances at the mess that is my hair and the edges of her lips rise, as though she suddenly realizes how hilarious I look. My relief is instant. I fucking hate seeing her upset. If I'd known my mom would've been disappointed with her then I would've just thrown the whole damn shampoo bottle out. Mom never really interferes much, and I thought this would be the same. I guess I look pretty damn ridiculous though. In hindsight, it'd be more surprising if she did let this go.

"Yes, okay," Emilia whispers. I turn around and kneel down in front of her while she rises to her knees on my bed. She shaves my hair carefully. Part of me was worried about putting a razor in her hands, but it seems my worry was groundless. She rests her hands on my shoulder and cups my neck as she works on me. I exhale in relief when she's done and pull away from her. When she's this close to me, it feels like I'm suffocating.

Emilia looks at me and I'm surprised when I see a brief flash of attraction in her eyes, followed by annoyance. I smile to myself. I don't have to look in the mirror to know my new hairdo suits me just fine. Her face tells me everything I need to know.

Chapter Four

EMILIA

I walk into my house to find it eerily silent yet again. We've been living here for years now, and it still doesn't feel like home. I feel more at home at the Clarke's. It's not exactly surprising either, since I spend more of my waking hours there than I do here. Thankfully, Helen wasn't too angry after last week's Nair prank. I hate it when she's mad at me. I would've hidden out in my house without a doubt, but luckily she's been acting like nothing happened. So has Carter — he hasn't retaliated yet, and I wonder if it's because he feels bad about Zach. I ran into Zach the other day, and he immediately made an excuse to get out of talking to me. I hope Carter feels terrible about ruining that for me.

I check my watch and bite down on my lip. It's almost nine pm. When we first moved here dad would always be home by the time I got back from dinner at the Clarke's, and every once in a while he'd actually come back to have dinner with me. When did things change? I think we've only been having dinner together once a month in the last two years. Recently he's been staying away until I'm already fast asleep.

My mood drops, and I walk towards the staircase. I miss him. I miss the way dad and I used to be. We used to hang out together, and he'd take me to eat junk food without my mom's permission. It's like I lost him when he lost my mother. I can't even remember the last time we really talked. It's like he stopped trying once he realized that I have Helen and Kate. Sometimes it feels like I'm a chore he puts up with. An unwanted reminder of my mother and the life he lost.

I jump when the front door opens with force. Dad walks in with a huge scowl on his face that transforms into pure anger when he spots me standing by the stairs.

"You're home," I say. He drops his briefcase to the floor and it pops open, a myriad of legal documents falling out. Looks like he's preparing for yet another case. He doesn't even glance at the papers. Instead, he's looking at me with barely contained rage. I have no idea what's wrong, but I'm certain I'm in trouble somehow.

"Emilia, do you want to explain to me why your mother called me to say you've been harassing her?"

My heart drops and I freeze. Harassing her? "I didn't," I retort. He narrows his eyes and stares me down the way I imagine he does criminals in court. I'm immediately intimidated. He is, after all, *the* John Parker, the public prosecutor that put a drug cartel behind bars a month ago.

"Did you send her countless emails and track her down on Facebook? She said you're stalking her. Is that true?"

My heart shatters. She called dad to say I'm stalking her? Why didn't she just reply to any of my emails? Why didn't she just tell me she wants nothing to do with me?

"Is it true?" he repeats.

I nod and then shake my head instead. "It's not like that, Dad. I found her profile on Facebook, and it had her email address on it. I just sent her a few emails to ask how she was doing."

My dad walks up to me. I've never seen him look so mad before, and definitely not at me. I don't understand what I've done wrong. Suddenly, he grabs my shoulders and shakes me. I'm so shocked, I don't even know how to respond. Dad has never acted this way before — he's never so much as punished me. It's always Helen that grounds me when I deserve it.

"Emilia, why won't you get it through your head? She left us," he shouts. "She wants nothing to do with either of us. Today was the first day I spoke to her in years, and it was because you've been harassing her! Are you crazy?" He's trembling, and the despair in his eyes is obvious. Just what did she say to him?

I bite down on my lip to keep from crying, but a tear drops down my cheek nonetheless. I've never felt this unwanted before. All I wanted was to talk to her. "Dad, I just wanted to know if she was happy. If she missed me. I thought maybe she'd want to see me..." I feel silly for wanting to reach out. I feel like a fool for missing my own mother.

Dad lets go of me and takes a step back. He pulls a hand through his hair, looking exhausted. When did he get this grey? He's thinner than he's ever been, and he's got bags underneath his eyes that never seem to go away. It's been seven years, but my dad looks like he's aged decades since my mother left. I wonder if the reason he loses himself in his work is because it allows him to forget about her — about *me*.

"She doesn't want to see you, Emilia. I wish it were different, but it is what it is. Promise me you won't contact her again. Why do you even want to speak to her at all?"

I sniff and look away. "I just miss her, dad. Why can't I miss my mom? Why is it so crazy that I might wonder if she misses me too?"

Dad sighs and shakes his head. "Honey, do you even remember her? She never even spent much time with you. What could you possibly be missing?"

I look down at my feet, unable to explain why I feel the way I do. He's right, I never spent much time with my mother. I'd usually be with a babysitter instead. But still, she's my mom. You only get one mother in life, and she's mine. I love Helen with all my heart, but she's not my mother, not truly. Yet if she can love me the way she clearly does, then surely my mother loves me even more?

"Dad, you're never here. You're always working and always pawning me off to the Clarke's. I love them, and they take great care of me, but they aren't my real family. You and Mom are. I'm always alone in the house or I'm at the Clarke's, and I miss having a family. Why shouldn't I get in touch with my own mother?"

Dad frowns and looks away, dismayed. "I'm never home because I work my damn ass off to provide for you, Emilia. When your mother left, she took half of everything I own. She took your damn college fund! The woman took your future away, and you still want to get in touch with her?"

I look at him in disbelief. Surely that isn't true. Even if they did split their assets evenly, I doubt she'd have asked for my college fund specifically, and even so, I know we're far from struggling. We're not as well off as before my parents divorced, but we're definitely not doing so bad either.

Dad shakes his head at me. "You're so ungrateful, Emilia. Just like Isabella. You're just like your mother."

He pushes past me and walks up the stairs. He'll undoubtedly disappear into his room for the rest of the night. Our conversation is clearly over. I sink to my knees on the floor and try my best to hold back my tears. I never meant to be ungrateful — I just wanted to talk to my mother. I just wanted to know if she ever thinks of me at all. If she regrets leaving me.

I stare at the front door. All I want to do is hide and burst into tears in private. I want to sob my heart out, and I don't want my dad to find out how hurt I am. I pick myself up off the floor and walk out, closing the door behind me silently.

Chapter Five

CARTER

I was studying at my desk when I spotted movement from my bedroom window. Someone is walking through Emilia's backyard. I frown and lean in closer to get a better look. It's her. Emilia walks straight to the hedge between our gardens and worms her way through it. Is she trying to sneak in to speak to Kate? Why would she be so stealthy about it?

I walk down the stairs in a rush and move towards the living room window to keep an eye on her. She isn't headed for the house at all. Instead, she walks straight towards the treehouse in the backyard. She pauses at the bottom of the stairs and looks up. She seems to hesitate, and I can't help but feel like something is wrong with her. She walks up slowly and holds onto the hand rail along the stairs as though it's all that's keeping her standing. I'm rarely genuinely worried about her, but tonight something seems off.

I wonder if I should get Kate to check up on her, but then I shake my head. If she wanted to talk to Kate, she would've just come into the house. It seems like she wants some peace and quiet, and while I'd love to respect her wishes and give that to her, I need to make sure that she's all right.

I glance up at the stairs. The house is quiet. I doubt my mom will realize if I sneak out for a bit. I nod to myself and make my way to the back door. I'm nervous as I walk to the treehouse. I look up at it, my eyes lingering on the sign Kate and I made. It used to read Kate and Carter's Treehouse, but Emilia stuck a bit of wood over it with her own name on it, so it now reads Kate and Emilia's Treehouse. Initially, I kept removing it, but she's far too persistent. That's one fight she actually ended up winning.

I walk up the stairs, the steps creaking slightly underneath my weight. I pause halfway up when I think I hear something. It's soft, but it's definitely the sound of crying. My heart clenches. Emilia is crying? I can count the amount of times I've seen her cry on one hand. What could've possibly happened to make her cry? Did she argue with Kate?

I walk up the remaining steps and pause by the entrance. Should I enter, or walk away and pretend I didn't realize? The sound of her sobbing intensifies and my mind is made up. I enter the treehouse and spot her lying down on the window seat. She's lying with her back towards me, her shoulders shaking. Each one of her sobs tears me apart. I walk up to her and ditch my flip-flops next to hers. She's crying so hard that she has yet to notice me. I sigh and lie down next to her. I spoon her and throw my arms around her, hugging her tightly. She gasps and freezes before turning around to face me. My heart aches when I see the countless tears on her tiny little face. She sniffs and looks into my eyes. She looks so incredibly lost and hurt.

Emilia grabs my t-shirt and holds onto it tightly, the fabric stretching in her fists. She sobs even louder, as though her heart is irreparably broken. I throw my arms around her and hug her, her body flush against mine. I stroke her back and don't say a word. I just lie there with her and pat her hair and her back, over and over again. She cries for what feels like hours, and a little bit of my heart chips away with every sob that escapes her lips.

Eventually she manages to calm herself down. She relaxes in my arms, her breathing still uneven. It's like she's choking on her sobs, and I hate that there's nothing I can do to make it stop. Emilia isn't much of a crier. She never has been, not even when we were younger, so it breaks my heart to find her crying like this. I don't want to see her in pain for a single second.

She pushes her face against my chest, and I tangle my hand into her hair. She seems to want me close, but she doesn't want me to see her. I guess I'm the last person she wants to be caught in a vulnerable state by. In the last couple of weeks, things have been more tense between us than usual. I guess I've messed with her a little too much. I've pushed her away just a little too far.

"Wanna talk about it?" I whisper.

She shakes her head and clenches my t-shirt in her hand. The fabric is soaking wet from all the tears she shed, and it's clinging to my skin. Nonetheless, I don't move a muscle. Emilia's breathing evens after a couple of minutes and she brazenly grabs my t-shirt to wipe away her remaining tears. I chuckle and shake my head, letting her do as she pleases. Eventually, she pulls away from me a little, her eyes red and her expression sullen.

I grab my t-shirt at the edges and pull it up and over my head before handing it to her. "You've already soaked it through, Emilia. Just use it and return it to me next time," I whisper. She looks startled and takes it from me. I lean back and watch her while she uses my t-shirt to wipe her face and her puffy red eyes. My minx isn't a pretty crier; she never has been. She's never been fake or half-hearted in anything she does.

"Come here," I whisper, opening my arms for her. She doesn't hesitate to throw herself back into my hold. I close my arms around her and she presses her nose against my bare chest while my hand finds its way back to her hair. She lies there in silence until she's finally breathing evenly again and stops shaking.

"I contacted my mom," she tells me eventually. I tense. That woman is straight up trouble. Any woman that can leave her own child for another man isn't worth a second thought in my books, but I get it. I get Emilia's need for a connection. I see the way she looks at my mom sometimes, and I saw how hurt she was when my mom was about to scold her over the Nair prank. It's the closest my mom has ever gotten to being disappointed in Emilia. It was different from her occasional half-hearted scoldings, and I saw how much it tore Emilia apart.

"My dad found out. Apparently, she called him saying that I was stalking her because I emailed her a few times and sent her a friend request on Facebook."

I nod and stroke her back as she tells me about her argument with her dad. She pauses multiple times to swallow down her tears.

When she's done talking, I'm filled with rage. Both her parents must be insane. How could her dad get so mad over something like this? If anything, he should've defended Emilia's actions. What kind of mother would accuse her own child of stalking her?

"Emilia, your dad was just tired and upset," I whisper. I have no idea what he was thinking, but my need to console Emilia is greater than my anger at his actions. "He didn't mean what he said. You're not ungrateful at all. You never get into trouble with anyone other than me, and your grades are consistently the highest in your class. I know how hard you work for that. I know his words hurt, but I promise you he didn't mean them. It's gotta be tough on him to hear from your mom again, and for it to be over something like this."

She's silent as she thinks my words over. I don't know what to say to her about her mom. I understand why she did what she did, even if I don't agree with her. I personally think Emilia shouldn't contact her mother either, but I can't say that to her without hurting her even further.

Eventually she pushes away from me and sits up. Her eyes roam over my body, as though she's only just realizing that I'm half naked. Her gaze lingers on my abs and she blushes as she moves away from me. She's so antsy and nervous all of a sudden that I can't help but grin. Too cute.

"I — uh... thank you," she stammers. It's like she's finally realizing how intimately entwined we've been. —

Emilia twists my t-shirt around in her hands, as though she's thinking of what to say. I sit up and drink her in. It's rare for me to find her looking so... sweet.

Emilia smiles at me before turning and fleeing, my t-shirt in her hands.

Chapter Six

CARTER

I glance at Emilia from across the cafeteria. She's been silent and subdued all week. I get why she's so upset, but Mom and Kate don't. They're worried about her, and she won't tell them what's wrong. I guess she might be a little embarrassed about the situation. How could she not be? How do you tell someone that your mother accused you of stalking her because you sent her a Facebook friend request? I get it, but my mom and Kate don't, and Kate especially is worried sick. As far as I know, Emilia has never kept anything from Kate, so this is a first. This is the first time my little sister is at a loss and unable to cheer up her best friend.

Kate's eyes meet mine and she looks so sorrowful that I'm tempted to tell her what happened, but I can't betray Emilia's trust like that. It looks like Kate is hurting right along with Emilia. I hate seeing both of my girls so unhappy. I thought Emilia would snap out of it eventually, but it's been a week and she's still so sad. There's no other way to describe Emilia's mood. She's heartbroken. I'll need to do something. I need to make this better somehow.

"What's wrong, man?" Asher asks. I turn to look at my best friend. He looks as worried as I do. "Is it the girls? They've been weird."

I sigh. Even Asher noticed, huh? Both of them have been awfully silent. Emilia hasn't pulled a single prank on me and Kate hasn't been secretly goading her to. "Yeah," I murmur. "It's the girls, it's Emilia. I'll fix it, though."

Asher's eyes move back to the table the girls are at and he sighs. I follow his gaze to find Emilia looking at us. Her eyes meet mine and the edges of her lips tip up in a polite smile. That's gotta be the first time I'd rather she glare at me than smile at me. I want to see her eyes flash. I can't stand seeing her looking so numb.

"What can I do to help?" Asher asks. I look at him through narrowed eyes. Since when does he care about Emilia? "Kate has been so quiet lately," he says. "Usually she hangs out with us and tries to annoy us, but she's been weird lately."

I exhale in relief. "Kate?" I repeat, relaxing instantly. It wasn't Emilia he was looking at. It was *Kate*. I should be a lot more worried about my best friend looking at my younger sister like a lovesick puppy, but I'm not. I'm just glad it wasn't Emilia. The mere idea of Asher with Emilia makes me feel uncomfortable.

Asher looks up at me, panicked. "I mean, Kate *and* Emilia. Usually they're around to bother us, right? They're *both* a bit weird."

I bite back a smile. How did I miss that he's got a thing for Kate? I'll need to keep an eye on them because my sister will likely trample all over his heart. I know he won't dare make a move on her, but I don't trust Kate as much as I trust Asher. She's getting more and more rebellious these days. She'd get with Asher just to mess with me.

"Hmm, yeah. I've got an idea. I think I know how to make this better, but I'll need to run to the store. How much time do we have left?" I check my watch and nod to myself. Ten minutes should be enough time. "Be right back," I tell Asher.

He takes in my wicked grin and shakes his head. "Don't get into trouble, dude. Coach will have your ass."

I shrug. If everything goes to plan, Coach will never even find out. I run to the store and grab the two things I need: a jar of oregano and freezer bags.

I walk out of the store with a smile on my face and empty the contents of the glass jar into the freezer bag and then rush back to school. I only have a few minutes to pull this off, but this should definitely get Emilia to snap out of the funk she's been in.

I walk straight to her locker with a wide grin on my face. This is my best idea yet. She's going to freak when she finds a bag of fake weed in her locker. I put in the code to her lock and frown when it won't open. Damn. She must've changed the code *again*. I check my watch and start rolling the numbers into different combinations. I try her birthday, Kate's, mom's, as well as parts of her phone number, house address and zip code. Usually it's one of those. I groan when none of them work and drop my forehead to her locker. My plan is going to fail if I can't figure out the code. I pause and straighten. What if her code is similar to mine? The one thing she thinks I'll never guess. I put in my own birthday and Emilia's locker springs open. I smile and put the fake weed right at the front. It'll fall out when she opens her locker, and I need to make sure I'm there to witness it. Better yet, to film it. I can just imagine the look on her face.

"Hey Carter, what are ya doing?" a high-pitched voice says behind me. I jump and turn around to find Jennifer staring at me. She's wearing her cheerleader outfit for no reason whatsoever. I know for a fact that they don't have practice today, because Kate and Emilia would've let me know. Much to my dismay, Emilia actually made it onto the cheerleading squad. Not that the competition is fierce in a town as tiny as Woodstock. I'm pretty sure anyone that auditions is automatically in. I was hoping Kate would quit soon, but that's not happening now that Emilia has joined her. I don't like my sister being around these little vipers.

Jennifer's already minuscule skirt is pulled up even higher

than usual, and she smiles at me seductively — or so she thinks. I groan inwardly. She's been fucking following me around ever since I made out with her at the last house party we both found ourselves at. She seems to be convinced that she can just wear me down and it'll happen again.

"Nothing," I say, smiling.

"I've been looking for you all over."

My eyes fall closed and I inhale deeply. "I know," I mutter. I've been trying to avoid her, but she's tenacious.

"We should hang out sometime," she says as she twirls one of her long blonde locks around her fingers.

I shake my head and smile tightly. "I don't think that's going to happen, Jennifer. I'm sorry about last time, I was just drunk, you know how it is."

She's the one that kept fetching me drinks and then pretty much jumped me when I was too drunk to even function properly. I feel no remorse for turning her down flat. If our roles were reversed, I'd be making sure she got home okay. I wouldn't be waiting for her to get so drunk that she isn't thinking clearly. Jennifer gives me psycho vibes. I close Emilia's locker, but she still manages to look inside it before the door shuts. She gasps and I inhale deeply, praying for patience.

"Oh, my god. *Emilia Parker* is a pothead? Who would've known... It's always the quiet ones you need to be worried about. I knew something was off about her. She always acts like a goody two shoes, but I knew it was just an act," she says excitedly.

I try to keep from rolling my eyes and shake my head. "She's not a pothead," I snap.

Jennifer nods. "I see, so she's just selling? Can I have some? I just want to try it once."

"It's just a joke, Jennifer. It's not real pot. Emilia would never do that, nor would I," I say through clenched teeth. She fucking infuriates me.

Jennifer frowns at me, and her eyes flash. "You two are awfully close, aren't you? Is she the reason you don't want to hang out with me?"

I shake my head and walk past her. I literally have no time to deal with her right now. "I'm late for class, gotta go," I shout, praying she won't follow me to the damn classroom.

Chapter Seven

EMILIA

I know I'm in trouble when the intercom system announces that I'm expected to make my way to the Principal's office immediately. Kate and I glance at each other and I shake my head, indicating that I have no idea what this might be about.

I walk towards the Principal's office with slow steps, dreading the inevitable. The pranks Carter and I pull on each other have gotten me detention before, but I've never once had to go to the Principal's office. Besides, I haven't done anything, so that can only mean one thing. Carter got me into trouble.

I walk in to find Carter and Helen both sitting in front of the Principal's desk. Our neighborhood police officer, Officer Oliver, is standing behind them and I'm suddenly terrified. What even happened?

"Emilia," Officer Oliver says. I've volunteered to help the police force with neighborhood initiatives before, and I've always liked Officer Oliver. He's the very picture of a sweet old man, yet he's the last person I want to see standing here. My stomach is in knots as I walk towards Helen. She looks just as confused as I do.

"We called your father, but he said Mrs. Clarke would act as your guardian in his absence," the Principal tells me. I nod. I don't think my dad has come to school even once this year, so that hardly surprises me.

Officer Oliver clears his throat and we all turn to look at him. "We got a report that a student was dealing drugs, Miss Parker. Would you please allow us to check your locker?"

"What?" I whisper, my heart racing, a frown creasing my face.

Carter groans and buries his face in his hands. "How many times do I need to tell you? It's just a prank. There are no drugs."

Officer Oliver nods, his expression carefully blank. "Miss Parker," he says. I nod and lead him to my locker in silence. What the hell did Carter do? My heart is beating wildly as I unlock my locker. The door opens and a translucent bag falls to the floor. Officer Oliver picks it up and holds it up for me to see.

"What is this, Miss Parker?"

I look at Carter with wide eyes, but he looks frustrated.

"For God's sake," he snaps. Helen grabs his arm and stares him down, her eyes filled with worry and disbelief.

"Just open it and smell it, *please*," Carter says. Officer Oliver raises his brow and does as Carter asks. His lips tug up at the edges ever so slightly before his usual expressionless look replaces it. He hands the bag to Helen and shakes his head. She frowns as she raises the bag to her nose and inhales. She looks both relieved and furious when she realizes what it is.

"Oregano," she snaps.

Officer Oliver smiles and looks down at his feet before facing us again. "We reviewed the video surveillance, and it looks like your son put this in Miss Parker's locker." He turns towards us with a stern expression. "No more of this, kids. The next time I'm called in over a prank, I'll be taking both of you with me to the station. I'll let you think about your actions in a holding cell. Trust me, you don't want that."

Helen nods and slaps Carter's arm.

He looks annoyed but nods too. "Yes, sir," he says.

Officer Oliver shakes his head and walks away, looking irked.

I exhale in relief and glare at Carter. "Oregano, *really*?"

He shrugs and smiles at me, but his smile drops off his face when the Principal turns towards us. "I am sick and tired of the nonsense you two get up to. You're both suspended for a week," he says, red in the face.

Helen gasps and shakes her head. "Oh no, Principal. It was just a joke. Surely you can just give them detention for a week?"

He glares at Helen and huffs. "Detention? They're already in detention *every week*. If she wasn't one of my top students and he wasn't a promising football star, I'd be expelling them both! Now get out of here." He storms away and leaves us standing with Helen. I'd take the Principal's anger over hers any day.

"You two are both grounded. One week in your rooms. No phone, no laptop, no TV. No nothing!" she yells.

She walks away and Carter and I look at each other, both of us annoyed. "I can't believe you!" I shout. I push against his chest and follow Helen.

Carter chuckles. I can't believe he finds this amusing. We're freaking suspended *and* grounded. I stop and turn back to face him.

"The police were involved, Carter. It *isn't* funny!" I yell, my cheeks burning.

Carter grins and looks away. "It was only Officer Oliver and he adores you. And it's a little funny," he says. "Besides, I never meant for the police to get involved. I just wanted to shock you a little."

I roll my eyes. "Well, they *did* get involved. Who the hell called them if it wasn't you?"

Carter hesitates, his expression darkening. "The only one that saw me put the bag in your locker was Jennifer. I clearly told her it was just a joke, though."

I walk up to him and push him again. "Jennifer? *Jennifer*? My cheering squad Jennifer? Why would she even do that?" I ask in disbelief. Carter looks away and my heart suddenly sinks.

"You... did you sleep with her?" I ask. "Is this some sort of revenge thing?"

He holds up his hands and looks at me with wide eyes. "No, Emilia. Shit. Do you think I sleep with fucking everyone?"

I glare at him. "You asshole. You definitely slept with her. Why else would she do this? The police never would've gotten involved if you weren't such a massive slut. You disgust me!"

My heart feels unsettled and my stomach twists. I knew he'd been messing around with the cheering squad, but until today at least I didn't know who he did or didn't sleep with. I can't believe it was Jennifer, of all people.

Carter looks hurt and for a moment I feel bad, but then I think of him with Jennifer and the mental image just fuels my fury.

"You think you're so cool because you sleep around with all the girls, but you're not. You're really not, Carter. Just because you're a guy doesn't mean you're not an effing slut. You're just *so* freaking gross!"

I storm away and leave him staring after me. Somehow, I'm more upset about Jennifer than the prank he pulled on me.

Chapter Eight

EMILIA

I'm still mad when I storm into my room. A whole week — I'll have to be in this damn room all week, all because Carter couldn't keep it in his pants. Helen definitely won't let me hang out with Kate in that time. I stand by my window and glare at Carter from my room. I can see into his bedroom easily from here. He's got his desk pushed up against the window and his bed behind it. Sometimes, if I'm really peering into his room and he's forgotten to close his curtains, I can see him lying in bed. Carter walks into his room and drops his bag to the floor. He immediately walks to his window and opens it.

"I'm sorry," he shouts. I glare at him and shut the curtains. I storm down the stairs and grab a box of expired eggs before making my way up again. I drag my curtains aside and push my window open. My movements catch Carter's attention, and he opens his own window too. He looks so relieved that I hesitate for a second. Then I shake my head and grab my slingshot from my desk drawer. Carter and I both have identical ones that we'd use to throw messages at each other before we got smartphones. I guess messages is overstating it a little — they were mostly insults, and every once in a while, some actual conversations.

I grab one of the eggs and aim for his window. I shoot as hard as I can, and the egg hits him right in the chest. It cracks against his favorite t-shirt, the yolk running down his body. He looks down at it in surprise. Before he has a chance to shield himself, I launch another one. This one hits him right in the stomach. He closes his window in a rush, and the third egg crashes against it. He stares at me and shakes his head. He looks me right in the eyes as he lifts his t-shirt, taking it off. Then he opens the window just slightly and sticks his arm out to clean the glass with his t-shirt before closing it again. He moves so quickly that I don't have a chance to throw an egg at his arm.

I grit my teeth and slam my window closed before yanking my curtains closed too. I jump into bed. My feelings are all over the place. I should be mad about the fake weed prank, but instead I'm mad about Jennifer. I never liked her — she's always mean to Kate and me and always acts like she's so much better than us just because she's been cheering for longer than we have. Why did it have to be her? The idea of Carter and her makes me feel uncomfortable. I've never seen him with anyone, but I've heard that he can get quite wild at all the parties Kate and I aren't allowed to attend. Despite that, I've never seen him kiss someone and I haven't so much as seen him hold a girl's hand. Logically, I know he's probably been with girls, though. After all, he's the school's quarterback, he's clever as hell and he's actually nice to anyone who isn't me. I've always ignored the rumors about him as best as I could, but this time I'm finding it impossible to get the mental image of Jennifer and Carter out of my head. My heart aches thinking of the two of them together.

My phone buzzes and I glare at it when I realize it's a text from Carter. I click on it and nearly drop my phone. He's sent me a photo that was clearly taken on his bed. He's lying down, shirtless, and his jeans are hanging low on his hips. I can see most of his upper body, and he's got a smug grin on his face. There are some stains from the eggs on his abs, and two small red marks on his skin. I stare at the photo. When did Carter get this muscular? I know football practice is pretty tough, but hot damn. I zoom in on his abs and stare at his body with wide eyes. I felt how strong he is when he held me in the treehouse, and I saw his abs then too, but I was so flustered and sad that I didn't *truly* notice. Not the way I notice them now, in the obscurity of my bedroom.

My phone buzzes again, and I drop it onto my face. I groan in pain and rub my forehead. I check my phone to find another text from Carter.

Devil: *I'm hurt.*

I roll my eyes. I know he isn't actually hurt, but I *am* surprised to see the bruises. I didn't think it'd hurt him much at all. Was I wrong? I feel just a tiny bit bad. I didn't mean to hurt him.

Devil: *I'm really hurt. Didn't you see the bruises?*

I purse my lips and ignore him. I'm so annoyed. Far more than usual. My phone buzzes again and I stare at it through narrowed eyes.

Devil: *Minx, I didn't sleep with her. I swear.*

I bite down on my lip. Is he lying to me? Does he have any reason to lie to me?

Emilia: *Why would she respond the way she did if you didn't sleep with her?*

Devil: *Fuck if I know. She's crazy. She kissed me at a party a few weeks ago. I was really drunk, so I let her. That's all.*

My heart aches. He kissed her. I knew something must've happened between them, but I'm hurt nonetheless. I shouldn't be.

Emilia: *So you got with her? You might not have slept with her, but you made out with her.*

Devil: *I'm sorry, Emilia*

Emilia: *You should be. If not for your slutty behavior, we wouldn't have gotten suspended.*

I stare at my screen. It looks like he's typing, but then he stops and starts all over again. It takes minutes before he actually messages me again.

Devil: *I know you won't believe this, but the rumors you're hearing about me aren't actually true. I haven't slept with anyone, Minx.*

I stare at my phone in disbelief. Surely he doesn't expect me to believe that he's still a virgin. He's seventeen. I know most guys his age are already doing it. Besides, I've been hearing rumors about him for almost two years now.

Devil: *I'm not a slut, Minx. Quite the opposite.*

I'm about to reply when I hear the front door slam downstairs. Footsteps rush up the stairs and Helen walks into my room with a furious look on her face. She holds her hand out and I reluctantly hand her my phone.

"I know this one technically wasn't your fault, Milly. Nonetheless, I'm punishing you both. I don't mind your little feud and your arguments, but it cannot interfere with school. Carter gets away with a lot because he's on the football team, but you'll need your scholarship, Milly. You're so close to getting a free ride to college. Rein in the pranks, okay?"

I nod. I know she's only looking out for me and I love her for it, but I do feel like I'm being punished unfairly. Helen grabs my laptop from my desk and takes it with her.

"I'll leave the TV downstairs, but I'm going to come in randomly and make sure you're in your room where you're meant to be. Don't try me, Emilia."

I sigh and fall back onto my bed as she walks back out, my portals to the world outside in her hands.

Chapter Nine

CARTER

I'm going stir crazy. My mother handed me a bunch of ridiculously boring books that I have to read for English class. No one actually reads them, and she knows it. We all just look up summaries and write our reports on those. But I guess *I* read them now. It's the only form of entertainment available to me.

I stare into Emilia's room and she looks just as frustrated as I do. She's seated at her desk, facing me. Her hair is loose and she hasn't changed out of her favorite pajamas in days now. She too was handed the books on her own required reading list, and she looks just as bored as I probably do. I grab a sheet of paper and write on it with large letters before pressing it to my window. It reads *I'm bored*.

I hold it up until she finally notices. Emilia looks at it and grins. She gets up from her desk and comes back with a stack of paper in her hands. She writes out a message and holds it up to her window.

Me too. It's your fault.

I grin wryly and grab another sheet of paper. I'll never live this one down. The police getting involved is a first for us, and we've both had to listen to my mom's endless berating. *I know. Lesson learned. Should we play a game?*

What lesson? Yes, sure, she holds up. I look away. I know what she wants me to say. She's stuck on the idea of me and Jennifer. I know she blames me for getting with that airhead, and I know that she's right. Me getting with Jennifer is exactly what got us into trouble, but part of me is hoping it's more than that. Part of me is hoping she might be feeling a little jealous.

For being promiscuous. Let's play hangman.

Emilia laughs, her face transforming. She looks beautiful when she laughs and my heart feels a little funny.

Wow. You learned a new word. Impressive. I'll start.

I roll my eyes. My grades are just as good as hers, and if things go to plan, I'll be able to get at least a partial academic scholarship, and if I'm really lucky, a partial football scholarship on top of it. Woodstock is too small of a town to get a full-ride football scholarship, though that won't stop me from trying.

Emilia draws out the game and I guess the letters. It only takes me a couple of minutes to figure out what the words are, and I feel myself blush. This freaking Minx. I regret telling her I'm a virgin. I'm not sure that knowledge is safe in her little hands.

Virgin Mary, I write out, guessing the words correctly. I stick the paper to my window with force and Emilia starts laughing again.

There you go. Taught you an analogy, she replies. I glare at her and look away, my cheeks burning.

I storm into my bathroom in an effort to hide from her. It's the only place she can't see from her bedroom. I should've just closed my curtains, but I don't want her to know how flustered I feel. I'm annoyed and embarrassed while I undress — I shouldn't have told her. She'll never ever let me live this down. No one knows I'm still a virgin. There are plenty of rumors circulating about me, and I've never bothered to correct them. They all just added to my notoriety. There are a bunch of girls I've made out with at house parties that Asher and I have attended, and for some reason many of them claim to have slept with me when they definitely haven't. I don't know why they do it, and I don't particularly care either, or at least I didn't. Not until I realized my Minx looks down on me for it.

I stand underneath the shower and lean back against the wall. My hands automatically wrap around my erection. Recently I've been getting hard just thinking about Emilia and there doesn't seem to be anything I can do about it. Even when I'm mad at her and she annoys me, she still makes me hard. She can't ever find out because she'd freaking murder me if she realized. I've become a pro at hiding it from her. More often than not, I have my boner pressed up against my waistband to hide it. Lately I'm nearly always hard around her, though. It's getting more and more difficult to hide just how attracted I am to her. I guess it's a blessing that she's so damn clueless. I'm pretty sure even Kate suspects how I feel, and she's only slightly less obtuse.

I stroke myself and imagine it's Emilia's hands instead of mine. It only takes me a minute to come and I feel guilty straight away. She'd probably feel disgusted if she knew what I was doing. I shouldn't be thinking of her like that, but I just can't help myself. No matter how hard I try, my thoughts always go back to her.

I walk out of the shower with my towel wrapped around my hips. I spot some movement from Emilia's window and peek into her room. She's standing just out of view, but her bright red pajama sleeve is giving her away. She's being a peeping tom, huh?

I think back to her choice of words during our game and scowl. I don't bother getting dressed and lock my door before dropping onto my bed. From this angle, I can see her standing by her window clearly, but she seems convinced that she's well hidden.

Very well. Let's show her I'm not a complete freaking virgin. I close my eyes, running a hand over my chest and down my body. I tug my towel loose but keep it in place. I'm hard again, but I'm nervous. I don't know what she'll think of me if I do this. I don't know how far to take this.

I slip my hand underneath the towel and take a quick, subtle peek at Emilia. She's still standing by the window and she's watching me with open lips. I smile to myself and tug a little more of my towel away. I palm myself and pump my fist up and down slowly. Knowing that she's watching me makes it all so much hotter. I just came in the shower, but I know I won't last long this time either.

Emilia moves closer, as though she wants to see better, not realizing that she's now in full view. I grin and tug the towel away entirely, giving her a show. I increase the pace and throw my arm over my face as I come, hiding my expression from her. My entire body jerks and I make a mess of my stomach. I wipe it away quickly, scared that it might disgust Emilia. I take a quick peek to find her standing in front of her window, her cheeks flushed and her eyes dark. I stand up and she snaps out of it, hiding herself in a rush. My little Minx enjoyed that show, it seems. I guess this week of suspension won't be so boring after all.

Chapter Ten

CARTER

I walk into the gym where the girls are practicing and check my watch. They should be finishing practice in about ten minutes. Perfect timing. My eyes find Emilia's immediately and her cheeks redden when she spots me. I bite back a grin as I pull my sweaty t-shirt over my head and let it fall to the floor as I walk to the stands to take a seat. Emilia's eyes are on me the entire way, and I chuckle when she does some sort of twist and stumbles because she's too focused on me. She blushes and forces her eyes back to her captain, but she doesn't last long before she's looking my way again. I put my arms behind my head, flexing my muscles.

Ever since we were suspended and Emilia watched me jack off, things have been different between us. She doesn't know that I know she saw, and she definitely doesn't know that I did it on purpose, but the way she acts around me is different now. She blushes when I'm too close to her and her eyes linger on my body in a way they never used to before. I found that I enjoy seeing her flustered far more than I enjoy seeing her pissed off. Since Mom would kill me if I dared pull a prank so soon after the whole fake weed debacle, I've been messing with Emilia in a different way instead.

I've been keeping my curtains open and I've been walking out of the shower with nothing but my towel on almost every day. And every single day, Emilia stands by her window, where she thinks I can't see her. The way she looks at me when she does that makes me wonder if she might feel the same way I do. If nothing else, she must find me at least attractive enough to drop whatever she's doing and watch me instead. I doubt I'm grossing her out — she'd just have closed her curtains if so.

I haven't treated her to another show yet, but I'm planning on it. I love watching her flushed cheeks and her glowing eyes. I love imagining that she's just a little bit turned on because of me. Emilia and Kate's practice wraps up, and they both run up to me. Emilia looks really fucking hot in her cheering outfit. I've never had a thing for cheerleaders, but I can see the appeal now that Emilia is one. I can't wait to have her with me at the next game. I can't wait to make her proud on the field, knowing she's right there watching me and cheering for me.

The girls walk up to me and I wrap my arms around both of them. Kate pulls away immediately, her face scrunching up in disgust, but Emilia lingers in my arms. I wrap my arm around her waist and pull her closer to me. She leans into me and drops her head to my shoulder. I can't resist and lean in to brush my lips over her ear, giving her the softest kiss, if you can call it that at all. She sighs happily and blushes slightly, but it's enough for me to realize she's affected by me.

"Ugh," Kate says. "You're so gross, Carter. Why didn't you shower after practice? Disgusting." She brushes her arms with her hands as though she can clean off my sweat that way. Emilia pulls away from me too, but she does so reluctantly.

"You're one to talk," I tell Kate. "You never shower after cheering practice, and you always reek too. Pot and kettle and all that shit."

Emilia rolls her eyes and walks towards the locker room.

Unlike Kate and I, Emilia always showers. Pretty sure it's because she's just a clean freak and hates messiness and dirt. She doesn't even smell, but I guess it makes her feel better, and it's not like she takes very long anyway. Kate jumps up to follow Emilia into the locker room and I sit back down. Mom used to pick Kate up while I'd drive myself and Emilia home, but now that Emilia has joined the cheering squad, I suddenly find myself much more interested in staying late to get some extra practice in.

I grab my phone and start scrolling through my social media feed as I wait for the girls. Emilia is usually quick, but Kate loves hanging back and chatting with the vipers she's calling her new friends. I don't like a single girl on the cheering squad, other than Emilia and Kate. I'm pretty sure Emilia doesn't like them either. She's just doing this for Kate.

I'm worried about Kate. She has never really had friends other than Emilia. Until recently she was quite introverted and she'd only really come alive around Emilia and me. I'm happy to see her becoming so outgoing all of a sudden, but I'm also worried about what brought it on and about the girls she's surrounding herself with. I know I can't say anything to her, though. If I so much as mention to her they might have wrong intentions in approaching her, she'll just snap and say I'm making things about me. And maybe I am. Maybe I'm wrong. God, I hope I am.

Some of the girls walk out of the locker room and make a beeline for me. I'm not sure what they did in there, because they're still in their cheering outfits. I recognize them as the two girls Kate has been hanging out with most: Gabby and Layla, I believe.

"Hey Carter," Gabby says. She walks right up to me and gets into my space. She puts her hand on my arm and I grit my teeth.

"Hi," Layla murmurs. She's far more demure and seems like she might actually be a half decent person. I'm not sure why she lets Gabby drag her around.

"It's *so* nice of you to wait for your sister every day. My brother would *never* do that for me. You're so nice to Kate," Gabby says. "You really are a good brother. I'm kinda jealous."

She giggles, but I fail to see what's so funny. "Actually, do you think Layla and I could come with? We were thinking of hanging out with Kate anyway. It's not healthy for her to spend all her time with Emilia. She needs some new friends, don't you think?"

I'm holding onto my patience by a thread. Who the hell does this girl think she is? Is her brain malfunctioning or something?

"If you agreed to hang out with Kate, then I'm sure you can arrange your own ride," I say, not playing along. Her expression falls, and it's obvious that she's not used to people not giving into her right away.

"Oh, uh... well, we're going to your house anyway. Surely it doesn't really matter if we tag along?"

She's not wrong, and usually I wouldn't have cared, but something about this girl just irritates me. I shrug. "I don't have enough space in my car," I lie. The five of us would fit just fine.

"Oh, well I guess we'll just see you at your house later then," Gabby says, her voice high pitched. Her good girl persona cracks just a little and she grits her teeth, revealing her annoyance at not getting her way. I smile to myself and shake my head.

"No, you won't. I have plans. I won't be home later." I'm lying, but she doesn't need to know that. I don't want to hang out with her at all. I don't even want her in my house. I have a feeling she's one of those weirdos that would sneak into my room. The only girl that I'll ever allow that type of batshit behavior from is Emilia. No one else.

"Oh, well... I guess we can come over tomorrow instead," she says, startled. I frown at her and look at her through narrowed eyes.

"What does it matter if I'm there or not? You're hanging out with my sister, right? Not with me. It doesn't matter if you come over tomorrow or the day after. You won't be spending any time with me."

I try to be as clear as I can be. This is exactly what I was worried about. I vaguely recall Gabby trying to hit on me before she became friends with Kate, and I have this sinking feeling she's befriended Kate to up her chances. She seems to have it in her mind that she and I should be together. The quarterback and the cheerleader. I'm not sure which teenage movie is playing in her head, but I'm not interested in playing along. Girls have been approaching Kate for years just to get to me when they don't even know me, and I'm sick and tired of it. I'm tired of Kate getting hurt because of yet another fake friend. I know how this ends.

Gabby's expression falls. "What?" she says. "You don't want to hang out with us? Why?"

I cross my arms and stare at her. "Why the hell would I? You're my sister's friend. Not mine."

She blinks at me, as though I've just said something absurd. "But you hang out with Emilia all the time. I've seen you two hang out together, even when Kate isn't there. When Kate is sick, you still drive Emilia to school. *She's* your sister's friend too."

I laugh. I can't help it. "Make no mistake," I tell her, my voice low. "Emilia is indeed Kate's friend, but she's also very much *mine*."

Gabby swallows hard and looks away, frustrated and angry. She shoots me a look that tells me she isn't going to give up easily, and I pull a hand through my hair. I can't believe I have to put up with this shit.

Chapter Eleven

EMILIA

"God, I'm so excited," Kate whispers. She's practically squealing. I want to be excited for her, but instead I'm just left feeling kind of sad. "Can you believe Gabby wants to hang out with me again? She's like, *the* most popular girl in school and she keeps wanting to hang out with *me*."

I nod as I pull on my jeans. All she's been talking about ever since she joined the cheering squad is Gabby. Gabby could simply smile at her and Kate would act like Gabby just extended her the greatest kindness. It's weird and I don't like it. I just don't like Gabby. I don't like the way she always acts like I'm not there. Would it really kill her to treat me a little bit nicely? I also don't like the way Kate changes around her. Am I just being jealous? Am I being possessive because I've always been Kate's best friend, and now I suddenly come second? I'm not really sure.

"She invited me to go to the shopping center tomorrow. I really can't wait. What should I even wear?" she mutters, lost in thought.

I frown. "Tomorrow? But tomorrow is marathon day," I

whisper. Kate and I catch up on all our shows in one go every Wednesday evening, because that's when the new episode of our favorite show used to air. It's been a tradition for years, and even when we're sick we never miss it. It's our little mid-week break. Helen allows it in return for us not watching too much TV on other weekdays. One time I was so sick that Carter had to carry me into their house, blankets and all, just so I wouldn't miss marathon day.

Kate pauses and looks at me, her brows scrunched up in anger. "Seriously, Emilia? It's just marathon day. We can always catch up on our shows the day after. Or, you know, just watch without me. I don't care."

I bite down on my lip and look away. She *doesn't care?* That's new. Last year I watched one episode without her because she was grounded and she didn't speak to me for weeks. Yet now she suddenly doesn't care?

"Uh, okay," I murmur. "I'll do that, I guess."

Kate nods and waves it off like it's nothing. She continues to gush about Gabby while I finish getting dressed. Not once does she consider inviting me along. I'd rather eat my left arm than voluntarily spend time with Gabby, but it would've been nice if Kate at least asked. I'm surprised she's in the locker room with me at all. After all, Gabby isn't in here. I have zero doubt that she's hanging around Carter the way she always does. Is that why he's been coming to watch us practice? Because he enjoys her attention? My heart drops at the thought of it.

In the first few weeks after Kate joined the cheering squad, we'd always just wait by the car or he'd drive us home and get Helen to pick Kate up later. Yet now he's suddenly always at our cheering practice, and I can't help but wonder if Gabby has something to do with it. Both Kate and Carter seem so taken with her. What am I missing? Why am I the only one that doesn't like her? Maybe I really am jealous.

Kate is practically skipping when we walk out of the locker room. Usually it pisses her off when her friends hang around

Carter, but I guess this time it's different, because she smiles when she sees Gabby and Carter together. It's almost like this time she's counting on Carter to bring her closer to Gabby. She runs up to them and I'm left behind by myself. I walk towards them slowly, wishing I could just walk home instead. I feel left out and I'm tired of feeling this way. It wasn't so bad when she first joined the cheering squad, but lately it's getting worse. I'm always the odd one out, the awkward one, the unpopular one. It's bad enough that I feel unwanted in my own home, but now I'm starting to feel unwanted around Kate too.

"Emilia?"

I turn around to find a tall blonde guy calling my name. He looks familiar, but I can't recall where I know him from. I frown and smile at him politely. He freezes and cups his neck.

"You don't remember me, do you?" he asks. I blush and shake my head, feeling somewhat embarrassed. He sighs and looks down at his shoes. "It's Anthony. Tony, from down the block?"

I look at him with wide eyes. "Tony?" I repeat in complete disbelief. He chuckles at my expression and nods. "I — wow. You... you look different," I stammer. He used to be really small, and to be honest, really snotty. "I didn't recognize you. I'm so sorry."

He shakes his head and smiles at me, his cheeks tinged pink. Tony has lived near me for years, and every once in a while he, Kate, Carter and I would hang out at the nearby playground. I haven't seen him in a while, though. He definitely doesn't look like the snotty little kid he used to be.

"We aren't in the same grade, so we don't share any classes, but I see you occasionally. Every time I see you I want to say hi, but you're usually so busy," he murmurs.

I frown. Tony and I go to the same school? How did I not know that? It makes sense, because why else would he be standing in the school gym? Besides, our town isn't exactly big. We have a grand total of two high schools to choose from. I don't think I've seen him in the halls even once, though. I suddenly feel even more embarrassed and stare down at my shoes awkwardly.

"I'm here to pick up my sister. Layla?"

I look up at him in surprise. "Layla is your sister?" I ask. "How come she never mentioned it?" I say more to myself than to him. Layla is even more of a wallflower than I am. She's quiet, but she's an incredibly good dancer. I don't think I've ever even had a real conversation with her. Even when she was younger, she never liked going outside, so we never really played with her growing up. We rarely even played with Tony, come to think of it.

"Ah, well yeah, she's my sister. I usually wait for her outside, but I saw you standing here and I just thought I'd come in and say hi."

Tony smiles shyly and I can't help but blush in return. He's acting all flustered and cute, and I don't know how to respond to that at all.

"I thought maybe we could catch up at some point?" he says, his voice so soft I barely even hear him. I nod and glance back at Kate, but she's so caught up in Gabby that I can't catch her attention.

"Maybe we could go see a movie or something tomorrow?" Tony says, and I blanch. Is he asking me out? I thought he meant he wanted to catch up with both Kate and me. My surprise must show, because his cheeks turn bright red and he looks away.

I look at Carter. How would he respond if I agreed to go out with Tony? I grit my teeth when I realize that all of his attention is on Gabby. My stomach twists uncomfortably and I'm instantly enraged. I turn back to Tony and look up at him.

"Yeah, sure. Why not?" I say.

Tony grins and exhales in relief. "Okay, great. I'll wait for you after school, and we can just leave together."

I nod, suddenly a little flustered. This is a date, isn't it? My first ever date.

Chapter Twelve

CARTER

I turn the shower off and inhale deeply. Why do I smell Emilia's sweet perfume? It's faint, but it's there, and it definitely wasn't there when I got into the shower. She's either been in my room while I was showering or she's still there. What is she pulling now?

I grin to myself and wrap my towel around my hips before walking out of my bathroom. She doesn't move quickly enough, and I see her dive behind my bed. I'm sure she thinks she's moving like a freaking ninja though. Too cute.

Now, what should I do? I could lie down on my bed and give her another one of those shows I know she loves, but I'm not sure I have the courage to do that. It's different when she's right there, and I think it'd be more awkward than sexy.

Instead, I walk around my bed, and Emilia crawls underneath it to hide from me. How does she even remotely think she's being stealthy? She's quiet, but not so quiet that I wouldn't notice her.

I bite down on my lip to keep from laughing and sit down on my bed. I sit on my knees and lean over the bed just enough to grab her legs. I pull her from underneath my bed and she squeals.

"Oh, shit!" she shouts. Emilia jumps out of my grip and turns towards the door, but I pull her back before she can make a run for it. She stumbles and falls into my arms. Before she has a chance to flee, I turn her over and pin her down on my bed.

"Now what do we have here?" I whisper, leaning over her. Emilia laughs and squirms underneath me. Her movements make her dress ride up and I'm hard instantly. She stills when she realizes what position we're in. I'm leaning over her, my body on full display, while she's flat on her back on my bed.

Her eyes roam over my body hungrily and she gulps. She tries to drag her eyes away, but she doesn't last more than a second before they're back on my chest again. Her cheeks redden and her breathing accelerates. Looks like my little Minx is affected by me. I've suspected it for some time, but I'm still secretly thrilled.

"What did you do, Minx?" I whisper. She grins wickedly and I grab her hands. I pin them down above her head and lower my body on top of her fully. She gasps and looks at me with wide eyes. "You...You're..." she whispers. My hard on is pressing against her stomach shamelessly. Instead of pulling away, she tilts her hips up to better align with mine. Does she realize what she's doing?

"I'm *what*?" I murmur, my face hovering above hers. Emilia arches her back and presses her chest into me. Her eyes darken and the way she looks at me does funny things to my heart.

"Carter," she whispers. My name sounds like a plea on her lips. I didn't think I could get any harder, but I was wrong. I subtly grind my hips against Emilia's and a small moan escapes her lips. She parts her legs slightly to get me closer, and I doubt she's even conscious of her movements.

"Tell me what you did, Minx."

She blinks, as though she doesn't know what I'm talking about, and I grin. Looks like my little Minx is struggling to focus. I wonder how she'll react if I tease her a little more. I rotate my hips against hers and her eyes fall closed. She lifts her hips and I push against her. Emilia moans softly and blinks, her eyes hazy with lust. Looks like the little shows I've been giving her have turned her on as much as they have me. Her body melts against mine.

"Not telling," she whispers.

I chuckle and shake my head. I lower my face to hers until my lips are hovering just above hers. I want to kiss her so badly. What would she taste like? Would she be as sweet as she smells?

"Hmm... I guess I'll have to torture the information out of you. What should I do, huh? What kind of prank could you possibly have pulled on me this time?"

Emilia shakes her head and grins victoriously. She hooks her leg over mine and pushes against me, as though she wants to push me off. I panic, worried that she wants to get away from me, and I let go of her.

She laughs and pushes against me until she's got me on my back. I'm surprised when she straddles me, sitting right on top of my dick. I'm so hard that my towel is tenting up, and Emilia giggles.

"Oh, Carter... who would've known that the devil had a sweet spot for me?" she whispers. I bite down on my lip and look at her. Her dress is bunched up around her waist and I can just about catch a glimpse of her black underwear. Her skin is flushed and her eyes are flashing with passion. She's teasing me, but I suspect she's just as turned on.

"Well, baby, who says I don't respond like this to every girl that sneaks into my bedroom while I'm in the shower?"

Emilia's expression drops, and a hint of insecurity replaces her former bravado. I regret my words instantly. My hands move to her hips and I hold her gingerly. She looks away and sits in my lap, frozen. The moment broken. So it bothers her to think that my reaction to her isn't exclusive to her, huh? I sigh and run my hand over her back.

"So, what did you do, Minx?" I whisper. She blinks as though she's only just remembering what she came here to do in the first place, and she laughs, her eyes twinkling. Whatever she did, it'll be a good one.

"Wouldn't you like to know?" she says, grinning. I'm relieved to see the smile back on her face and put my arms behind my back. I lie back while Emilia sits on top of me like it's the most normal thing in the world. She's far more brazen than I thought she'd be, and I freaking love it. She doesn't even seem to feel self-conscious because of my hard on. If anything, she seems to revel in it.

"You do this often, Minx?" I murmur, an annoying thought crossing my mind. "Climbing on top of guys that are half naked and rock hard?"

Her cheeks turn bright red, and she looks at me with wide eyes. I bite back a smile. I'm enjoying this far too much.

"I mean, if you want, I can always remove the towel."

I didn't think she could get any redder, but she does. Emilia looks flustered and shocked, but why doesn't she look repulsed? She glares at me and I wrap my hands around her tiny waist. She's so beautiful. It's unreal.

I shift on my bed and feel something underneath me, almost like a marble. I frown and reach under my back, only to find that whatever it is, it's underneath my sheets. Emilia grins and jumps off me as I reach underneath my blankets. My fingers wrap around something that feels an awful lot like an insect, and my heart drops. She *knows* I fucking hate insects. I raise my hand to my face with wide eyes and a pounding heart. My panic must be obvious because she bursts out laughing and makes a run for the door.

I'm so shocked by the cockroach in my hand that I can't even stop her from leaving. I drop it, staring at it in horror. Emilia's phone camera flashes from my peripheral vision and then she's gone.

I stare at the horrendous thing on my bed in utter shock. It takes me a full five minutes to realize it isn't even real. I pick it back up with trembling hands and shake my head. This girl... she'll be the death of me.

Chapter Thirteen

EMILIA

I rush out of the house, munching on my breakfast bar with half my books still in my arms instead of in my bag. I know that damn devil is going to leave me behind if I don't hurry. He's done it to Kate before, and I don't doubt that he'll do it to me too if I give him the chance. Ever since he got his license and his car last year he's become even more insufferable. I know he's going to want payback for the cockroach prank too. I'd be a fool to give him an excuse.

Carter is leaning against his car, arms crossed and eyes on his watch. He's wearing dark jeans with a black tee that looks far too good on him. My eyes roam over his body and linger on his crotch. I feel myself blush, my mind flashing back to the way I sat in his lap yesterday. What was I even thinking? I can't believe I behaved that way. I just can't think straight when it comes to Carter.

Ever since we were suspended together, I've turned into a nympho of sorts. I can't stop thinking about him and the way he touched himself. I can't help but wonder what he'll feel like against me and what he might feel like in my hands. I keep peeking into his bedroom like the pervert I've become. In the weeks since our suspension, I haven't seen him touch himself the way he did then, but he keeps forgetting to close his curtains and walks around half naked all the time. It's a sight I enjoy far too much. Would he be embarrassed if he found out I've been watching him? Would he think I'm weird? I can't look at him without my thoughts turning indecent.

Carter glances up from his watch and I snap out of it. I jump into the car and glare at Kate, who's occupying the back seat.

"I don't understand why we can't both sit in the back," I snap, reviving our daily argument. Carter leans over and his cologne washes over me. Whatever he's wearing smells delicious on him. My heart starts racing and I blush when he grabs my seatbelt and buckles me in.

"For the last time, Minx. I'm not your damn driver. One of you is sitting in the front or neither one of you is coming with me."

I roll my eyes and cross my arms over my chest. Kate puts her hand on my seat and leans in as far as her seatbelt allows her to. "So, are you excited for your date?" she asks.

My head whips towards her, and I look at her with wide eyes. I shake my head frantically to indicate that she needs to shut up, but she glances at me and then at Carter with a wide smile on her face.

"What date?" Carter asks, his tone sharp.

I shake my head and sit up straight. I look out the window and try to hide my crimson cheeks. "She's kidding," I tell him. I see his hands tighten on his steering wheel from my peripheral vision and I bite down on my lip. He can't find out. If Carter finds out, he'll find a way to ruin the first date I've ever been asked on. I can't let that happen. Most of the girls in my class have done far more than date, and I've never even been kissed yet. If it's up to Carter, I never will be.

Besides, it's both his and Kate's fault I agreed to the date in the first place. Kate is hanging out with Gabby later, and I can't seem to get Carter off my mind these days. I don't like it at all. Every time I get lost in thought, I wind up thinking about him.

"What date?" he repeats, his voice low and dangerous. I know that voice. He only ever sounds that way when I'm really, really close to snapping his patience. I bite down on my lip and stare out the window. If I just refuse to answer, he'll eventually let it go. He knows from experience that I'll only talk if I want to.

"Oh, Tony asked her out. I can't believe it took him this long to finally ask. He's been crazy about Milly for years now, but she barely realized he even existed. I'm so excited!" Kate says. She bounces in her seat, ignoring the death stare I'm giving her from the mirror. She leans back into her seat, looking pleased. I shake my head, shocked by her betrayal. How could she do this to me? She *knows* Carter is going to fuck this up for me now.

"Tony who? Tony fucking Andrews?" Carter says. He looks at me, his eyes blazing.

I shrug. "None of your damn business," I reply, fuming. Carter clenches his jaw and stares straight ahead. It's silent for a couple of minutes.

"No," Carter says eventually. I frown and look at him in question. "You can't go. I forbid it," he says angrily.

I burst out laughing. "You *forbid* it?" I repeat, my hackles raised. This asshole. "Who do you think you are, Carter? You're not my dad. I'm going, whether you like it or not."

"No, you're fucking not, Emilia," he yells. He looks furious, which is really unlike him. Carter has his dad's patience. He never gets mad and he never really snaps at me, but it looks like he can't help it today. The idea of me going out with Tony really pisses him off.

"When?" he asks. Kate looks from me to him with wide eyes, as though even she didn't expect his anger. "Catherine, when?"

She hesitates and then answers him truthfully. "Uh, today, after school." I cross my arms over my chest and ignore both of them the rest of the way. Carter sighs as he parks the car and leans over me to undo my seatbelt, but I slap his hand away.

"I'm not a fucking child, Carter. I can do it myself."

I storm out of the car and then walk back petulantly a minute later. Carter holds up my bag with an infuriating smile on his face and I snatch it from him. I glare at him and then turn, storming off all over again.

Kate runs after me, but I ignore her. "Come on, Milly, don't be mad. I'm sorry."

I stop and turn around to face her. "How could you do that to me, Kate? You're supposed to be my friend. My *best* friend. You know he's going to ruin my date now, you *know* he will."

Kate sighs and pushes my hair behind my ear. "I wasn't thinking... I just figured he'd find out one way or another. I just thought it'd be good for him to know that you're into Tony," she says.

I look at her, confused. "What?" I'm not even that into Tony, and she knows it. I only said yes because I've never been asked out before and I thought it might be fun to catch up with Tony. I guess part of me wanted to see how Carter would respond though. Kate shakes her head and smiles, but her smile doesn't reach her eyes.

"It's nothing, Milly. I'm sorry. Come on, we're going to be late for class."

I nod, and she takes my hand as we rush to our classroom. I sit down in my usual seat, feeling totally out of it. I'm not even sure why I'm feeling so disgruntled.

Mr. Fields goes down his attendance list and eventually asks for our homework. I jump and grab my bag. I spent all night finishing it because I it totally slipped my mind. If not for Kate, I would've definitely come in empty-handed today.

I frown when I can't find it. I know I put it in my bag, I'm a hundred percent sure. I even double checked this morning.

My mind automatically replays this morning's events and I

grit my teeth just as my phone buzzes. I take it out of my bag and check the text message.

Devil: *Looking for your essay?*

"Fucking Carter," I mumble under my breath. Kate looks at me with raised brows. "He *stole* my damn essay."

Kate bites down on her lips but totally fails to hide her amusement.

"Funny for you. He never does this shit to you," I snap.

"Emilia," my teacher says, pausing in front of me.

I look up at him apologetically. "I forgot it at home, Mr. Fields. I swear I did the essay. I just don't have it on me."

He looks at me and sighs. I was sure he'd let it go — I'm top of my class and I've never forgotten to hand in an assessment, but he shakes his head. "You know the rules, Emilia. Detention."

I groan and drop my head to my desk. That asshole. He's trying to make me late for my date, and he's succeeding. Tony and I were meant to leave school together today.

Chapter Fourteen

CARTER

I've been fucking pissed off all day. Fucking Tony Andrews. How dare he ask her out? I made it clear to everyone that Kate and Emilia are off-limits. He sure has some goddamn balls. And Emilia. I can't believe she's going on a date after the moment we had yesterday. Was it just me that thought her sitting in my lap the way she did was, I don't know, *something*. I slam my locker closed and make my way to the exit. I managed to take Kate home and get some extra weight lifting in while waiting for Emilia, but she should be done with detention any time now.

I'm even more pissed off when I see Tony standing by the door. He's obviously waiting for her. His eyes widen when he sees me and he straightens. What she sees in him is beyond me. He's stick thin and dorky as hell. Is that her type?

I walk up to him and pause right in front of him, getting all into his space. "I heard you asked Emilia out," I say, my voice soft and low. Tony gulps and then nods. How brave. "Pretty sure I made it clear to everyone that my sister and Emilia are off-limits. You have a hearing problem, bud?"

He shakes his head and opens his lips, only to close them again. "She — she isn't, Emilia isn't... she isn't your sister," he stammers. "If she wants to go out with me, she... she can."

I laugh. "I fucking know she isn't my sister, Andrews. Thank fuck she isn't. Still doesn't mean you get to ask her out. What should I do with you, huh?"

The door opens, and Emilia comes rushing out. She looks fucking stunning. Her blonde hair is pin straight, as though she flat ironed it, and her top looks far tighter and far lower than it looked this morning. Guess that explains her absence at lunch. I stare at her cleavage and then glare at her. All this is for Tony? She walks up to me and pushes me away, getting between me and Tony. My opinion of Tony sinks even deeper when he lets her. Why the hell is he hiding behind Emilia?

"Tony can take me home later," she says. "You didn't need to wait for me."

She grabs Tony's hand and drags him away, pushing past me. He follows her eagerly. I huff and trail behind her, glaring at their joint hands the entire time. It's obvious that they're walking towards the shopping center a few blocks down. Movie theatre it is, then.

Emilia keeps glancing back and obviously knows I'm following her, but she ignores me. Fine by me. I stand behind them in line when we reach the movie theatre and buy myself a ticket for the same movie they're watching. I watch Emilia's agitation rise and grin to myself. I'm sure at some point she's going to snap and cuss me out. Let's see how Tony likes her then.

I wait for them to enter the theatre and follow them in. Once they're seated, I take the seat to Emilia's left while Tony is on her right. She's stuck right between us. If it were up to me, I'd have gotten between her and Tony, but I'm sure she'd throw a fit if I tried.

Emilia tenses and glares at me, but I keep my eyes on the screen as I munch on my popcorn. I have no idea what movie we're even watching. I just asked the girl at the ticket office for one ticket for whatever Emilia was watching, but it'll probably be a chick flick.

Eventually Emilia acknowledges me and elbows me, hard. "Get lost," she murmurs. I turn towards her and take in her face. She's fucking wearing mascara or some shit. She dressed up for this fucker, huh? Like she needs it.

"Nope," I say, popping the p just to piss her off. She turns away from me and grabs Tony's hand. It's clear that they want to move seats, but the room is packed. I watch them whisper to each other, and eventually they settle down in their seats, obviously having realized that they have no other choice.

Tony keeps her hand in his and I lean over her to glare at him, getting right in his puny little face. "You better keep your hands to yourself if you want to *keep them*," I tell him, my voice soft and low. I smile at him and he shudders. He looks at me with wide eyes and lets go of Emilia's hand. She glares at me and I hate that she actually looks distraught. Surely she doesn't really care about this weasel?

Emilia leans into me and grabs my bicep, her grip tight. "Don't do this to me, Carter. *Please*. I've never been on a date before, not even once. I've never even walked around holding hands with a boy. I'll be sixteen soon and I still haven't even been kissed. All because you scare everyone away."

I look into her eyes and smile. "Good," I whisper, intensely pleased with her words.

She shakes her head and looks up at me pleadingly. "Please don't do this to me, Carter. It's so unfair," she says, her voice breaking. My heart fucking shatters. She wraps her arms around herself and stares up at the screen, looking lost as hell. I hate that I did this to her. Am I being too harsh? Realistically, I shouldn't be so strict with her. I know Kate has managed to sneak a couple of dates in that she thinks I don't know about, and I let that go. So why can't I let it go when it's Emilia?

Emilia looks crestfallen as we walk out of the movie theatre. Tony looks at her awkwardly and then comes up with an excuse to leave. She nods at him in understanding and sighs, a small insincere smile on her lips.

She stares at him as he walks off and I hate it. She looks like she's freaking pining after him. Tony, of all guys. Eventually she inhales deeply and starts walking back to school. I follow her silently. She doesn't look up at me until she reaches my car. I unlock the doors and she gets in. When I sit down, she turns towards me, her eyes blazing.

"You went too far, Carter. It's one thing to pull pranks on me, but this was downright unacceptable. I never interfere with your private life that way. I don't cock block you when you're flirting with girls. Don't think I didn't notice how you were all over Gabby the other day. Did I act the way you just did? No. I just let you be. Why can't you do the same?"

I stare at her wide eyed. "When the fuck was I all over Gabby?" I ask her, outraged. Hell will freeze over before I'm ever all over that viper.

Emilia rolls her eyes. "That's not the point, asshole. I've never interfered with your flirting and whatever, but you've done it twice now. Once with Zach and now with Tony. It's not okay."

I lean back in my seat and start the car. I'm not even sure what to say to that. She seems genuinely hurt. I wasn't really thinking today at all. All I knew was that I didn't want her going out with Tony. Was I being too mean to her?

"I'm going to make you pay for this," she says when I fail to respond.

"Yeah, I know, Minx," I murmur. I'm relieved she's speaking to me at all. When Emilia gets really mad, she gives me the silent treatment. I can't stand it when she does that. I'd rather she fight with me and cuss me out than treat me like I'm thin air.

She stares at her phone the entire way home, and it isn't until much later that I find out why. My little Minx texted everyone we know saying I have fucking chlamydia.

Chapter Fifteen

EMILIA

"Are you sure you don't want to join us, John?" Carter and Kate's dad asks, like he does every year. And like every year, my dad shakes his head resolutely. "No, but thank you for offering, William. And thank you for taking Emilia with you."

He nods at William and smiles at me. "Have fun, sweetie," he says. Things have been awkward between Dad and me lately. He hasn't apologized for the way he snapped at me a few months ago, but he's been coming home earlier and he's been having dinner with me when he can. If he can't make it home, he'll call me to have a chat instead. I guess that's better than an apology, but I would've liked to have both. I smile back at him and make my way to the car. As I approach, Carter and Kate both shout, "shotgun not middle seat!"

I groan and squeeze in between them. The journey to their summer cabin is a couple of hours and I'm going to be so uncomfortable between Kate and Carter. Besides, I've done my best to ignore Carter since he pulled that stunt on my first date. I haven't forgiven him yet, and I don't plan on being nice to him any time soon.

Carter's thigh is pushed against mine and much to my surprise, he shifts away from me, edging closer to the door. I frown and lean back in my seat. I cross my arms over my chest, intent on giving him the silent treatment.

"I'm so excited!" Kate squeals. "I can't wait to go swimming and kayaking at the lake. I wanna tan as well," she tells me. Usually I'd be just as excited as her. Towards the end of the school year we usually go to the cabin one weekend a month, and if William can get some time off, we usually go for a week during summer break too. Our weekends at the cabin are normally the highlight of our summer, but this time I'm too annoyed with Carter to enjoy it.

I can't believe he ruined my date like that. He might pretend like he's never seeing anyone, but I know he's lying. The other day I heard Gemma gossiping about how he took her to our local coffee shop to hang out. He's such a hypocrite. I hate that he goes on dates *all the time* while I can't even go on *one*. Just the idea of Carter with other girls pisses me off. If *he* gets to do it, then I do too. If Carter gets things his way, I'll die a virgin. I don't want that. I want to date just like other girls my age, the way Carter seems to.

"Aren't you excited?" Kate asks. She pushes against my arms, inadvertently pushing me closer to Carter.

"Yeah, yeah. I'm excited," I say eventually, my voice dripping with sarcasm.

Kate frowns at me, her smile dropping. She leans forward and glares at Carter and me. "You two better not ruin this for me. I don't know what the deal is with you this time, but you're both being weird. You don't usually fight for this long."

Carter crosses his arms over his chest and looks out the window, ignoring her. Helen turns around to look at us with raised brows.

"Kate is right. You usually get over your little arguments quite quickly, but you've barely spoken in two weeks now. What is going on with you two?"

I stare down at my hands, hoping she'll just let it go, but she won't.

"Emilia?" she says, her tone sharp. I glare at Carter and then look back at Helen.

"He ruined my first date," I say. "Tony asked me out, and we went to the movies. Carter *followed* us there. He even sat right next to me and told Tony he'd lose his hands if he touched me. Tony didn't even dare hold my *hand*," I tell her, distraught all over again. I didn't even want to go on a date with Tony, but it was the first time I'd ever been asked out. I still wanted it to be a nice experience.

Helen stares at Carter with wide eyes. "You didn't!" she says, outraged. She stares Carter down and he looks away. He purses his lips in annoyance and I'm glad I got him into at least a little bit of trouble. Helen looks back at me and raises her brows. "And you. You went out with Tony? Little snotty Tony from down the block? The one that would always cry if anyone so much as touched him?"

I feel myself blush. "He's not little anymore," I say. Carter snickers and turns his head towards me.

"Yeah he is. Puny little fucker."

Helen shoots him a warning look and Carter grits his teeth. "You were totally out of line there, Carter. If I hear of you behaving that way towards Emilia again, I won't hesitate to ground you. Pulling pranks on her is one thing, but ruining her date is something else entirely."

She then turns to me, a stern look adorning her face. "And you, Emilia, I thought we had an agreement that there would be no dating until you and Kate turn sixteen. There are still a few months left until then, isn't that right?"

I sigh and nod. Carter chuckles and I elbow him.

"I'd better not hear any more of this dating nonsense until you're sixteen," she tells me. I pout and eventually nod.

Carter grins and I pinch his thigh, making him yelp. He grabs my hand and brings it to his lips, biting down on my finger. He doesn't bite hard, but it's still annoying as hell. I gasp and lean in, biting down on the arm he's holding me with.

Helen turns back around, looking exasperated. "You two aren't kids anymore, for god's sake. Behave, or we're turning this car around and you can both stay home!"

I glare at him and let go, and he glares at me just as fiercely. I don't remember the last time I've been this mad at him. Kate looks worried and pats my leg. "Don't piss mom off," she warns me. "You know how crazy she gets when she's mad."

I nod. It's true. Helen has the patience of a saint, but when she snaps, all hell breaks loose. I stay quiet for the remainder of the journey, and so does Carter. I don't think the trip to the cabin has ever been so peaceful. Even William looks surprised with our behavior.

As soon as we're out of the car, Carter and I both storm into the cabin, ignoring each other. He's the one that's in the wrong, so I don't know why he's acting so aggrieved. He should be apologizing to me, but instead he's just making me even more angry.

Chapter Sixteen

CARTER

I walk behind Emilia as we hike through the woods like we do every year. She hasn't spoken a word to me in hours and I hate it. I can't believe she's acting like this over *Tony*. I could've sworn she didn't even remember him until recently. Besides, if she just called him and asked him out, he'd be falling all over himself to take her on a second date.

Kate glares at me as though it's her I've wronged. It irritates me that she's more concerned with Emilia and I ruining her weekend than she is concerned *about* Emilia. It's very rare for Emilia to be angry for long. She forgives and forgets quickly, but this time it's different. It's been almost two weeks. She hasn't even been peering into my bedroom lately. Instead, she's been keeping her curtains closed. She won't speak to me on the ride to and from school either. It's frustrating as hell.

I fall into step with her and she glances up before looking away again. I hate how easily she dismisses me. I can't remember the last time I was angry at her for more than a day. I don't think I ever have been.

"Are you looking forward to going kayaking later?" I ask, grinning. I still remember how she toppled over last year. I ended up having to dive into the lake to help her. It was hilarious.

Emilia doesn't even glance at me. She just increases her pace and starts walking next to my mother. Mom looks behind her curiously and raises her brow at me, but I shake my head. I didn't do anything, not today.

Kate punches me in the arm and glares at me. "I can't believe you did that, Carter. She's never going to forgive you for ruining her date with Tony. And she shouldn't either. Tony is super cute and you totally embarrassed her in front of him."

I groan. "I guess cute is a good way to describe him. He's small and dainty, like a kitten. Seriously, though, Kate. He's just some little prick. Surely she doesn't actually like him."

Kate rolls her eyes. "She does. Or she did, anyway, until you ruined it. Why would she go out with him if she didn't like him? Tony is smart and sweet. He's super tall too. What's not to like?"

I roll my eyes. "Sounds like it's you who likes him, and not Emilia."

Kate blushes and looks away. "I can't believe you actually followed her into the movie theatre. What's wrong with you? I know you two have that whole feud thing going on, but that was a bit weird. It wasn't even really a prank. Why did you do that?"

I grit my teeth. I don't know why I did it either. Up until now I've been okay keeping my feelings to myself. I didn't think I'd ever act on them, but I could barely think straight when I realized Emilia was actually going out with someone else. I couldn't help it. I don't know what to say to Kate. I don't have a reply for her. Not an acceptable one, anyway.

"Lately, the way you two act around each other is a bit odd too. I can't quite put my finger on it, but something is weird. And then the thing with Tony... Kind of seemed like you were jealous or something. But you'd never go there with Emilia, right? She's part of our family. She's like our sister."

Her words hit me right in the gut. Is that how Emilia sees me?

Does she see me as a brother? No, surely not. If she did, she wouldn't watch me the way she does. She wouldn't have climbed on top of me and sat on my dick if she saw me as her *brother*. I definitely don't see her as a sister — not even close.

Kate hits my arm again. "I'm serious, Carter. She's not someone you can mess with. She's my best friend, she's part of our family. I'd never forgive you if you made a move on her. I know she's pretty. *Everyone* thinks she's pretty. I see how all the boys around us look at her... but not you, okay? Please, Carter, not you too."

I'm startled by her words. Emilia and I don't even flirt. Not really. Every once in a while I catch her looking at me with interest, but it's always fleeting. What is Kate seeing that I'm not?

"I don't know what you're talking about," I say. Kate sighs and shakes her head.

"I'm not blind, Carter. When you think she's not looking, your eyes are always on her. Sometimes it feels like you treat her even better than you treat me. When I have a late class, you make Mom pick me up, but when it's Emilia, you always go get her yourself. I've been on the cheering squad for months now, but you only started showing up at training once Emilia joined. No matter how much I begged you to come hang out with me and the girls, you'd never do it. But now Emilia joins and all of a sudden you show up? I'm not stupid."

I blink in surprise. I didn't even realize I did any of those things. I guess it's true, though. I did start showing up to her cheering practice specifically because I wanted to come watch and mess with Emilia. Looks like Kate is far more observant than I gave her credit for.

"I don't get it," I reply. "There's nothing going on between me and her, but even if there was, how is that at all your problem?"

I'm irrationally angry. I know she's not being unreasonable, but I still don't like hearing it. Kate looks up at me pleadingly.

"She's my best friend, Carter. She's at our house almost every day and she comes with us on every trip. We spend all our holidays together too. Imagine if something happened between you two? How awkward would things get? I don't want to lose my best friend because of you. Besides, I've seen the way she looks at you sometimes. Just stay away from her, okay?"

I glare at her and grit my teeth. "She's my friend too, Kate. We both met her at the exact same time. It's not like you've known her any longer. You don't own her. If anything happened between us, then that's none of your business at all."

Kate's expression crumples and I instantly feel bad. I sigh and throw my arm around my little sister. "Nothing is going on between me and her, Kate. I understand where you're coming from, but I promise you, you're worrying for nothing. She and I are just friends. Or frenemies, I guess. That's a thing, right?"

Kate laughs and nods. "Yeah, that's a thing. I just hope you'll never be more than that, Carter. You might not care, but I'm dead serious. I'll never ever forgive you."

Such harsh words coming out of my sweet baby sister's lips are shocking to say the least. I never realized she felt so strongly about this. I never realized she was worried about Emilia and me getting together.

"I hear you, baby sis. You're worried for nothing, though. Like I said, *nothing* is going on between Emilia and me."

Kate shakes her head. "You say that, but I see the way you look at her. I see the way she looks at you too. Don't do this to me, okay? Don't fall for her. I love Emilia too, so I get it, but she's already every teacher's *and* Mom's favorite. Why does she have to be yours too?"

I'm startled to say the least. "Kate, surely you aren't jealous of Emilia? She won't ever take your place, you know that, right? Even if I did ever date her, and I'm not saying I will, but even if I did, you'd still always be my only sister. Nothing would ever change. And mom doesn't love her more than she loves either of us, of course she doesn't. It's just that you and I both hate doing chores, and Emilia is always helping Mom with one thing or another. I think Mom also gives her just a touch more attention because her dad is literally never there for her."

Part of me resents Kate for begrudging Emilia the little bit of attention my mom gives her, but part of me also gets it. Kate probably feels like she's always had to compete with Emilia, and in most aspects she loses. Not because she isn't as good as Emilia, but because Emilia works much harder than Kate ever does. Emilia has better grades because she works her ass off for them. While Kate is usually on her phone or watching Netflix, Emilia is usually studying. She works even harder than I do, and I'm putting absolutely everything into getting an academic scholarship. It's true that Emilia gets more of Mom's attention, but that's because she's always helping around the house and she's always offering to go everywhere with Mom.

"I don't care," Kate says. "You just can't go there with her. Not her. Anyone but her, Carter."

I'm not sure what to do. It might very well be too late for me to take a step back.

Chapter Seventeen

CARTER

Emilia *still* hasn't spoken a single word to me. I thought for sure she'd get over it because we're at the cabin and it's usually her favorite place to be, but she *hasn't* gotten over it. I can't believe the first time we're truly arguing is over freaking Tony. He's not worthy of touching a single strand of her hair. If it was someone worthwhile, I'd at least understand it - I think.

I pace back and forth in my room. I need to make this right somehow, but I don't know how. Eventually, I come up with an idea that might work.

I walk up to the room she shares with Kate and knock. Kate opens the door and looks surprised to find me standing here. I push past her and walk into the room. Emilia is sitting on their bed in a tight t-shirt and some very short shorts. No bra. I can see the outline of her nipples right through the fabric and force my eyes up.

"What're *you* doing here?" she snaps. I grab her hand and pull her up. "Let's have a chat," I tell her. She tries to pull her hand out of mine, but I won't let her. Kate jumps up to follow us, but I shake my head and glare at her.

"Give us some time to talk things out. You can have her back later. Or do you want us to keep arguing and ruin the rest of the weekend?"

Kate looks conflicted and sends me a warning look that I ignore. If she knew what I'm about to do, she'd never let Emilia go with me. Part of me feels guilty for doing something I know she'd vehemently oppose, but I can't resist. I've been brooding all night and I cannot stay away from Emilia. I can't leave things be the way they are.

I drag Emilia along and out of the house. When she stops resisting, I intertwine our fingers and hold her hand, my pace slowing. She follows me to the lake. Neither one of us speaks when we get to the little makeshift pier where the water is shallowest. Eventually I turn towards Emilia, her hand still in mine. I raise our joined hands to my heart and look into her eyes.

"I'm sorry, Emilia."

She looks surprised and blinks up at me. She seems torn. I know she wants to stay mad at me, but she can't. "You're such a hypocrite," she snaps. She pulls her hand out of mine and wraps her arms around herself. The move only pushes her chest out more.

"Hypocrite?" I repeat. She nods and glares at me.

"Yes, *hypocrite*. I know you go on dates all the time. Matter of fact, Gemma told me you took her to a coffee shop to 'hang out' last week," she says, air quoting the words. I bite back a smile.

"Minx, what exactly did you think hanging out meant? Gemma and I were working on a project together. I asked to meet her so we could finally *finish* it."

She looks at me in disbelief, and the stubborn tilt of her chin tells me nothing I say will convince her I didn't actually go on a date with Gemma. Hell, I've never bothered to go on a date with anyone, but she won't ever take my word for it so I don't bother telling her.

I pull a hand through my hair and sigh. "Okay, Minx. How about a clean slate? I'm sorry. Can we stop arguing, please? I hate arguing with you. You know, like really arguing. I really am sorry. I didn't mean to hurt you. I never mean to hurt you, Emilia. I was just *being me*."

She purses her lips and eventually nods at me. "Was it really that hard to just apologize?" she asks. I drop my head and sigh.

"You never apologized, you know. You ruined the first date I ever went on, and you didn't even bother to say sorry."

That's what she's so upset about? She's upset because I didn't apologize? I bite down on my lip and nod contritely. "You're right, Minx. I didn't even realize, but it's true. I didn't apologize. I just assumed that you knew I was sorry. And, you know, I kind of just didn't really get why you were so upset about Tony. Him, really? He doesn't deserve to so much as look at you, Emilia."

She blushes and looks up at me with wide eyes. "It's not him I was upset about, per se," she whispers.

I sigh and twirl a strand of her hair around my finger. "Then what was it?"

Emilia looks away, her cheeks bright red. "Carter, that was my first date. I might not have cared that much about Tony, but I was still excited. And now all I'll remember about my first date is how bad it was."

I shake my head and place my hands around her shoulders. "That wasn't your first date, Minx. It wasn't a real date. Let me make it up to you, okay? Truce?"

Emilia smiles. "Yeah, okay. Truce," she whispers.

I exhale in relief. I was worried I'd have to do far more groveling, and I have no idea what the right thing to do would be.

"Okay, great, so can we swim now?" I ask, smiling down at her.

She looks at me in surprise. "Swim?" she repeats.

I nod and tip my head to the lake behind me. I'm hoping this might make up for the date I ruined.

"It's evening, Carter. We can barely see. Surely we shouldn't be going into the lake right now."

I grin mischievously. "What, you don't dare go skinny dipping?" I pull my t-shirt over my head and let it fall to the floor. My hands move to the button on my jeans and her eyes are glued to my fingers. Fucking hell, I'm hard already.

"Turn around," I tell her. She swallows hard and looks at my body longingly. She's undressing me with her eyes. I doubt she knows what she's doing to me when she looks at me like that. Emilia nods and turns around, and I undress quickly. I hesitate, but end up taking my boxer shorts off too. I drop them on top of my jeans so she'll know I'm actually naked.

I rush to jump into the water. I was hoping it'd be colder so I could at least get rid of my damn hard on, but no such luck. I turn my back towards Emilia. "Okay, your turn, Minx."

Part of me is worried that she'll change her mind and walk off, leaving me here naked by myself. Or worse, that she'll walk off with my clothes — I wouldn't put it past her.

I breathe a sigh of relief when I hear fabric hitting the floor. Emilia lowers herself into the water far more gracefully than I did, and suddenly I'm nervous as hell.

"Hmm, I thought you'd chicken out," I say, my voice trembling slightly.

Emilia glares as she swims towards me. "I would never."

I'm startled when she grabs my shoulders. I'm tall enough to stand here, but Emilia isn't. She uses me to keep herself afloat and her body is far too close to mine. All I can think about is that she's naked and my heart starts racing. The tips of my shoulders are above the water, and the way Emilia holds herself up allows me to just about see the top of her breasts. She's so stunning.

"How come you wanted to go swimming?" she asks.

"Skinny dipping was on my bucket list," I murmur. "Besides, I heard that it makes for a cool, unique date. It's the only thing I could come up with on such short notice and with no time to prepare."

She looks at me in surprise and smiles. "This is a date?" she asks. I shrug and brush her wet hair out of her face. She sees right through me. "You wanted to make up for the date you ruined?"

I look away when she grins at me. I'm blushing and I'm hoping it's too dark for her to tell. Emilia smiles and pulls herself closer to me. My arms wrap around her instinctively and without thinking I pull her flush against me. We both freeze when our bodies touch. My erection is pressing up against her stomach and her breasts are crushed against my chest. Her lips fall open and she looks shocked, but she doesn't move away.

"Emilia," I whisper. She looks up at me nervously and wraps her arms around my neck clumsily.

"You said this is a date, right?" she whispers. I nod and bite down on my lip. I never would've even been able to imagine that Emilia might act this seductively. Her gaze moves to my lips and back to my eyes. "Will you show me what I've been missing out on?"

My hands move to her ass and my dick twitches when I grab a handful of her delicious curves. Emilia gasps and then giggles, tightening her grip on me.

"Emilia, what are you saying?"

My heart is racing, and my mind is whirling. I wanted to give her a unique first date, but this is beyond even my wildest imagination. Emilia hesitates and then leans in. She kisses the edge of my lips. All it'd take for her lips to be on mine is a slight turn of my head.

"What's bringing this on?" I whisper. She pulls away from me, surprised. Her eyes suddenly fill with insecurity and she tenses in my arms.

"I — I mean, I thought you said this was a date," she says, her voice high and flustered.

I blink. "Do you want *me*, or do you just want to experience what it's like to date?"

Emilia looks at me and hesitates before answering. "Both," she whispers.

I tighten my grip on her ass and grab her harder. "What does that mean, Emilia? Does that mean you would've kissed fucking Tony if I'd left you alone with him?"

Her face scrunches up in disgust at the thought of it, and though she tries her best to school her features, she fails. I chuckle and relax.

"I guess that's a no," I say. She pouts and looks away. "I need you to tell me what you want, Emilia. I need to be sure we're on the same page here."

She groans and buries her hands in my hair. She pulls slightly, trying to make her annoyance known. Her cheeks are bright red and her blue eyes are sparkling. She's never looked more beautiful than she does in this moment.

She pulls my head closer suddenly, catching me by surprise. My lips slam against hers and our teeth clang together.

"Ouch," she murmurs, pulling back. She rubs her lips and looks away in frustration. She seems embarrassed at her failed attempt to kiss me and pushes against my chest. I chuckle and move one of my hands into her hair.

I gently pull her back to me until my lips are hovering over hers. She squirms in my arms, and I smile. I tilt my head and brush my lips against hers, once, twice... She sighs and I lean in. I kiss her carefully and gently. She melts against me. I brush my tongue over her lips and she opens up for me. Before long, she gets the hang of it and starts kissing me back properly, her clumsiness waning.

She hesitates for a second, and then she wraps her legs around my hips. My dick is pushing right up against her. One wrong move and I could probably slip inside her. I've never been so stressed out and turned on at the same time. She writhes against me, grinding her hips against mine. My dick slides against her with every move and she moans. She kisses me more frantically and tangles her tongue with mine as she increases the friction between us. I need to tell her to stop. I need to tell her I'm going to come if she keeps moving like that, but she won't let me pull away. She's moving against me passionately, moaning between every kiss. Emilia looks hot as hell and I'm struggling like crazy to hold on. The tip of my dick slides against her just right, and her entire body contracts over and over again.

I pull my lips away from hers to watch her fall apart, and it's the most glorious thing I've ever seen. She looks beautiful and so incredibly sexy as she looks into my eyes, wave after wave of pleasure rocking her body. I can't hold on. I lift her up higher as I come, trying my best to keep her from realizing. Her lips fall open and she's breathing hard. When her body finally relaxes, she smiles at me knowingly. I feel myself blush and drop my forehead against hers.

"Okay... that's not how a date usually goes, baby. I don't think things are supposed to move so quickly," I whisper. I guess it was inevitable for us. We never do things half-heartedly.

Emilia bites down on her lip and rests her head on my shoulder, her lips pressed against my neck. We stay wrapped up in each other like that for a while, and I hug her tightly.

"Emilia," I whisper. She looks up at me. I can't quite get the words out. I want to ask her whether she likes me the way I think she does and whether she wants me as badly as she seems to.

"I — I just... uh — you have... you have no idea how long I've wanted to do that," I stammer.

Emilia smiles and bites down on her lip. "Me too," she whispers. My heart hammers in my chest and I'm filled with elation.

"Really?"

Emilia nods and hides her face in my neck. I chuckle and pull her closer, closing my arms around her.

"How long?" I ask. She sighs and presses a soft kiss against my skin.

"Months, Carter. I've been wondering what it'd be like to kiss you for months now."

I can barely believe it. I've been teasing her and messing with her for months, and I knew she wanted me after the way she sat in my lap, but still, to finally hear her say it sets my heart at ease. I bury my hand in her hair and tighten my grip on her. It's like I can't get her close enough.

"We need to go back, Minx," I say reluctantly. "You know Kate will send a freaking search party out if we stay away for too long."

She groans and nods in dismay. "I want to stay a bit longer," she whispers. I smile and kiss her forehead.

"Okay, baby. Just a little while longer."

Chapter Eighteen

CARTER

I wake up the next day to find the cabin empty. I glance at the clock and groan. It's 11am, so everyone will already be hanging out at the lake.

Emilia and I got back in late last night. Neither one of us wanted the night to end. All I was planning on doing last night was apologizing and creating a memory with her that we'd always share. I guess I wanted to be her first date, as she was mine. I'm not sure when my feelings for Emilia even started to change.

I smile to myself and walk into the bathroom. I'm so giddy with excitement and I'm so eager to see her again. I get ready in record time and race towards the part of the lake with the embankment, the bit we always use as a beach.

Looks like they've already set out beach recliners and I'm relieved to find a spare one for me set up. I didn't think to bring one. I look at the set-up and grin to myself. The spare seat is right at the edge, next to Emilia.

"Morning," I shout, a wide smile on my face.

My mother looks at me suspiciously. "So, you *are* alive. I wasn't sure when you refused to get up this morning."

I cup the back of my neck and grin at her.

"What were you doing last night? Were you playing video games again?" she asks.

I nod and walk towards my beach chair. Emilia tenses when I approach, and I try my best to keep my eyes off her body. Fucking hell, though. She looks hot in that minuscule white bikini of hers. Last night I got to feel her curves, but I didn't get to see them. When we got out of the water, she forced me to turn my back to her, so I was left to imagine what her curves might look like. The bits of her body that her bikini doesn't cover are magnificent. I'm sure she wasn't *that* busty a year ago.

Her eyes drop to my crotch and I look down with wide eyes. How the hell did I not realize that I've got a boner? I plop down on the beach recliner face first and end up crushing my dick painfully. I groan and Emilia chuckles, her cheeks flushed. She keeps peeking at me while pretending to read her book. After a couple of minutes, she gives up on trying to be subtle and outright ogles me. I glance at my parents, but they're absorbed in each other, and Kate is napping. I reach into my swim shorts and adjust my erection to hide it better. Emilia's eyes follow my every movement.

"Wanna go for a swim?" I ask. "Race you there."

Emilia chuckles and throws her book onto her chair. I take off running and she's not far behind me. When I'm certain that we're out of view, I stop and turn around. Emilia almost crashes into me. She's smiling and panting when I grab her by her waist and pull her closer, my lips finding hers. She kisses me back and I lift her into my arms. Her legs wrap around my waist and I walk us towards the trees and towards my secret place.

"Where are we going?" she asks, before she sucks down on my lower lip. She drives me insane.

"You'll see."

I carry her into the small clearing and place her down on the grass gently before joining her. She giggles and pulls me on top of her. She's eager to have her lips back on mine, and I'm relieved that she wants this as much as I do. She was clumsy yesterday, but the way she's kissing me today drives me wild. I roll my hips against hers, and despite the amount of clothes between us, I'm already close to coming.

Emilia parts her legs to get me closer and I move my lips towards her neck. She groans when my erection isn't right where she wants it anymore, and I chuckle against her skin. I kiss her neck softly and then nip at her collarbone, hesitating before moving lower. Emilia pushes her chest out in a silent bid for more. I look up to find her watching me with lust filled eyes. I smile and place my lips against the top of her breast, trailing a path down slowly. She squirms underneath me, her breathing uneven.

When my I graze her nipple over the fabric, she moans softly. I look up at her again and gently tug on her bikini top. I place my lips against her skin and she arches her back to push more into my mouth. I smile and suck down on her nipple. She moans and throws her leg around mine. She's sensitive. I've read that some women are and some aren't, but it looks like my Minx is *very* sensitive. I tug on the string that keeps her bikini top together and it falls open, revealing her breasts. I inhale sharply and Emilia moves to cover herself.

"You're gorgeous, baby. So beautiful," I whisper. I kiss her hands until she finally moves them away and reveals what she's hiding underneath. I move back up and kiss her while my thumb teases her breast. She grinds against me and I push my forehead against hers.

"I can't hold it when you do that, baby. You're driving me crazy, Emilia."

I lower my lips to hers and kiss her. She lifts her hips up to get the angle just right and I give her what she wants. She moves her hips against me quicker and quicker until her body twitches and her head falls back. She moans and I smother the sounds she's making with my lips, my own release not far away.

I collapse on top of her and bury my face in her neck, both of us panting. "That was amazing," I whisper. Emilia turns her head and I pull back just a little to look at her.

"You weren't lying?" she asks. I frown, unsure of what she's talking about. "You said you've never slept with anyone," she murmurs. She looks petulant and cute as hell. I grin and peck her lips.

"Hmm, I didn't lie, Minx. I'm a virgin," I tell her awkwardly. Emilia blushes and nods at me.

"I'm glad," she whispers.

We both freeze when we hear Kate's voice nearby.

"Milly," she shouts. "Carter, where are youuu?"

Emilia pushes me away and ties the strings of her bikini top in record time. She looks at me, panicked.

"Oh god. *Kate.* Oh, my god, what were we even thinking? Shit. We can't do this," she says, her voice trembling. I look at her with wide eyes, my heart dropping.

"No, it's fine. It's okay." I say. I know Kate warned me away from Emilia, but when it comes down to it, she'll eventually get over it. So long as Emilia wants me, there's nothing and no one that I'll allow to stand in our way. Kate loves Emilia to bits. There's no way that she won't want us to be happy together.

Emilia shakes her head and pushes me away. "Shit. What's wrong with us? This can't happen again, Carter. Kate is my best friend — I *cannot* mess around with her brother. That's *so* against the girl code. She'd never forgive me! I love your mother so much and they'd *both* be horrified if they found out. They'd feel like I betrayed their trust."

She starts to panic and even though my heart is shattering, I grab her shoulders and try my best to ground her. "Hey, breathe, baby. It's alright. We don't need to tell them if you don't want them to know."

Emilia shakes her head. "No. Let's just pretend nothing ever happened. It was just some making out, anyway. It's not like we actually dated or anything. Please, Carter."

I stare at her in disbelief and then look away, unable to face her. The last twenty-four hours have meant the world to me. I thought we were on the same page. Was this just a fling to her? Was she just trying to figure out what she's been missing out on?

"I understand," I murmur, smiling tightly. I don't understand, but for Emilia I'll pretend.

Chapter Nineteen

EMILIA

Kate looks worried when I make it back to the embankment. "Hey, where were you?" she asks. Helen looks me over and narrows her eyes before looking away.

"Oh, Carter and I went for a swim." I reply. "I guess maybe we went a bit too far out?"

Kate nods and sits back down, her eyes studying me carefully.

"Your bikini isn't wet. Your hair isn't either," she remarks.

I look at her with wide eyes. "I... I... uh, I put my hair up so it wouldn't get wet, and my bikini dried on the walk back," I stammer. I'm being so suspicious but I can't help it. I've never had to lie to Kate before. I can't even look her in the eye. She'd be so disappointed if she knew what Carter and I were getting up to.

Carter walks up to us, looking annoyed as hell. William glances at him and grins. "Had a good swim, son?" he asks. Carter looks startled for a second and then nods, keeping his eyes to the floor. He brushes past me and sinks down on his chair. Kate looks from me to him and frowns.

"You guys argued again, didn't you?"

I bite down on my lip and shake my head. "No. I guess, maybe a little."

Kate rolls her eyes. "You two were literally together for an hour or so. How the hell did you manage to fall out again in that time? Don't go around ignoring each other again, because it's awkward as hell."

I nod, feeling immense guilt. Whatever happens between Carter and me will definitely impact my friendship with Kate. I can't risk it, no matter how much I want to. "I'm sorry," I whisper. She looks surprised and Carter sits up to glare at both of us.

"I don't ever fucking complain when you two are arguing or refuse to speak to each other. Last year you didn't speak to each other for a whole goddamn week because one of you watched the series finale of some dumb show without the other. Did I fucking complain? No, I didn't. So why the hell are you now concerned with whether Emilia and I are arguing? It's not like that's new to you."

Helen looks like she might intervene but then decides to stay out of it, much to my surprise. Kate jumps out of her seat and stares Carter down. "Emilia is *my* best friend, Carter. Of course I'm concerned about it. I hate it when you two put me in a difficult position. I hate it when I have to choose a side to be on."

Carter grits his teeth and storms off while I bury my face in my hands. I'm racked with guilt. What was I thinking, getting with Carter like that? Things got out of hand so quickly too. Kate is right, of course. I can't put her in a position where she'd ever have to choose between me and Carter.

"Ugh," she yells, storming off in the other direction. I stare at the woods that Carter disappeared into and bite down on my lip as I make my mind up. I want to follow him so badly, but I can't. I need to put Kate first. I inhale deeply and run after her.

"Hey, wait up," I shout. Kate pauses and turns. She wipes away her tears and my heart starts to hurt. I'm feeling beyond guilty. I stopped thinking when I was alone with Carter. I didn't think about Kate at all. All I could think about in the moment was that I wanted Carter — that I've wanted him for months now.

I open my arms and she crashes into them. I pet her back as tears stream down her face. "I... I hate arguing with him," she says.

"I know, Kate." She might act all tough, but I know better than anyone that she adores Carter. He's the one person she's always looked up to. "It's okay," I whisper. "It's such a minor argument. It's fine."

Kate pulls back and shakes her head. "It's not. You don't understand, I — " She inhales deeply and shakes her head. "It's nothing," she whispers. I wipe away her tears with my thumbs and she looks up at me gratefully. It hurts to see her so upset. It hurts even more to know that I'm the root cause of it.

"I'm so mad," she whispers.

I laugh and throw my arm around her. "Yeah, Carter tends to have that effect on people. Welcome to my world, girl."

She laughs, and I'm instantly relieved. Kate and I walk around hand in hand, swinging our arms like when we were kids. I can tell she's gathering up the courage to tell me something, and I'm wondering if she's going to warn me away from Carter. My heart sinks at the thought of her issuing me an ultimatum like that. I don't know if I could even keep my word if she asked it of me. It's getting harder and harder to resist Carter, to pretend like I don't feel anything for him.

"There's something I want to ask you," she murmurs eventually. She sits down at a little bench along the road and looks up at me with an anxious expression. "Do you like Carter?"

I freeze. I'm not sure what led her to ask me this, and I'm not sure what to say to her. I've never kept anything from Kate, and it seems wrong not to tell her now.

"I — Carter... I — " I can't manage to get the words out and keep stammering. My heart is beating so loudly that it feels like it's trying to claw its way out of my chest.

"You don't, right? You wouldn't do that to me, would you, Milly? Carter and you have always hated each other. That hasn't

89

changed right?" Kate says, her voice high pitched and borderline panicked. I swallow hard and stand in front of her, frozen and nervous as hell.

"I... no, I don't hate him. Of course I don't hate him," I say.

Kate looks up at me pleadingly.

"I see you as my sister, Milly. I've always given you everything I could and I've always invited you to every family gathering we have, including our weekends at the cabin," she says, waving her arms around and gesturing to the lake behind us. "I share my Mom with you and never complain when the two of you hang out together when you're supposed to be *my* friend. My Dad offered to teach you how to drive despite it meaning that he'd have less time to teach *me*, and I didn't complain. I never complain, Milly."

I nod and look down at my shoes, racked with guilt. She's right, she has always shared every single thing with me, and she's never once complained.

"But not Carter, Emilia. You can't ever go there with him unless you're willing to walk away from our friendship. I won't stand back and watch you two ruin everything. My Mom will never get over it if you two date and break up, or if you two even argue and you refuse to come over for dinner. I won't let you hurt her like that. Our friendship wouldn't be the same anymore either. I refuse to suffer through you two avoiding each other and fighting with each other, which you definitely would do if you ever dated. I don't ever want to have to pick a side to be on, and with the way you two argue right now, I'd definitely end up having to choose."

I shake my head and hold my hands up. "I'd never hurt you or Helen, you know that, Kate. I'd never do that."

Kate shakes her head and laughs wryly. "You say that, but the way you two fought during this trip has hurt us all. Mom was worried when you two fought in the car and the entire hike was awkward as hell because you two wouldn't speak to each other. Even Dad asked me what was going on between you and Carter, and if you'd be okay. We'd all have had a better time if you didn't come with us at all, Emilia. Surely you see that that's what things would be like if you and Carter ever dated? I'm dead serious, Milly. If you go there with Carter, our friendship is over. I won't ever forgive you."

I bite down on my lip as hard as I can to keep my emotions in check. I didn't realize I was hurting everyone with my actions. I only meant to fight with Carter, but Kate is right, every fight we have does affect his family. Usually our fights aren't very serious, so they're easy to ignore, but it wouldn't be the same if we dated. I can't do that to the Clarkes. I'll have to stay away from Carter.

"I understand, Kate," I say, my voice shaking. My heart feels shattered and I feel like crying. Why does it feel like I just lost Carter forever? I already knew he and I could never be together, but it's still painful as hell to know I'd stand to lose everything if I followed my heart.

Chapter Twenty

EMILIA

I'm late. I couldn't sleep last night and only ended up falling asleep three hours ago. I kept thinking about Carter and the things we did at the cabin, the way the weekend ended and how I wish things were different. Just thinking about the way he kissed me turns me on, and thinking about the look on his face when I told him to forget what happened tears me apart. Then there's Kate and the things she said to me. I can't even fault her for asking me what she did.

Carter is standing in front of his car and looks up when I walk out. His eyes roam over my hair and my outfit before he looks away. I wore an extra tight top and paired it with a tight skirt that makes my ass look amazing. I'm surprised when he doesn't check me out.

Instead, he gets into the car, ignoring me. I'm startled and suddenly feel unsettled. He's being weird. I open the passenger door and he shakes his head as I'm about to get in.

"Just sit in the back with Kate."

He looks back at the steering wheel and starts the car.

"I thought you said you don't like feeling like you're our driver," I say.

Carter huffs. "What's the point in pretending like I'm not? That's exactly what I am to you two, right? A driver. Would you be in my car every morning otherwise? Just get in the back, Emilia."

I tense and look at Kate with wide eyes before getting in the back seat. She frowns and shakes her head — looks like she doesn't know what's up with him either. Carter drives us to school in silence.

"What's going on?" Kate asks, her brows scrunched up. Carter tightens his grip on the steering wheel.

"This is what you wanted, isn't it, Kate? You wanted Emilia and I to stop fighting. We have."

Kate rolls her eyes. "Thank god, no more daily arguments about who gets to sit in the front. Can't believe it took you this long to give in," she mutters. Carter looks at her in the rear-view mirror and nods.

"Yep. Let's just pretend it never happened," he says.

I bite down on my lip and look out the window. I don't like the way he's behaving, but I can't fault him for it either. He isn't doing anything I can actually complain about. He's just being... off.

He parks his car when we get to school and rushes off without us. Usually he'd walk us to class and ask about our plans for the day. Kate looks as startled as I do.

I watch as Gemma intercepts him when he reaches the entrance. She's in his class and she clearly has a thing for him. I hate that he smiles at her so brightly when he didn't so much as look at me today. She touches his arm as they talk and the way she pushes her breasts out for him annoys me. His eyes drop to her chest and jealousy twists my stomach. Her breasts are far bigger than mine and the low-cut top she's wearing showcases them perfectly. Even I can't deny that Gemma is beautiful. She flirts with Carter endlessly, and he lets her. I didn't realize until today that I've never actually *seen him* flirt with anyone. I've heard rumors, but I've never witnessed it myself. He's always kept a polite distance from the girls at school if Kate and I were present.

Carter moves closer to her and she looks up at him seductively. I bite down on my lip hard and walk past them, trying my best to pretend like I don't care when my heart is shattering. Kate glances at me but doesn't say a thing. I know I wasn't very subtle, but she seems to think my jealousy might just be a bad mood. She's right and I cannot go there with Carter, but I didn't think it'd hurt so much to see him with someone else.

I'm pissed off during class. My mind keeps replaying the scene I witnessed this morning. The way he looked at her chest and the way she touched his arm. How close they stood to each other. If that's how he discusses school projects, then it's no wonder there are so many rumors about him. I somehow thought that what happened at the cabin was special to both of us, but now I'm wondering if I'm just another girl he's hooked up with.

"You've been quiet all morning. What's wrong?" Kate asks. I follow her to the cafeteria and shake my head.

"It's nothing. I couldn't sleep last night, I'm so exhausted," I reply. It isn't a lie, but it isn't the whole truth either. I hate having to keep things from Kate, but I can't tell her I hooked up with her brother. Not after what she said to me at the cabin.

Kate freezes when we search for a table, our trays in hand. Her eyes zero in on Carter and Asher's table. They're notorious for always having lunch together and not wanting to socialize with anyone else, but today there are two girls sitting with them. I recognize Gemma, and I think the other girl is Chloe. Just like this morning, Carter and Gemma are totally absorbed in each other. Much to my surprise, Asher seems to be talking to Chloe. I rarely see him with girls. He's usually as unapproachable as Carter.

Kate walks towards their table with a grave expression on her face and slams her tray down with force, some of her food going flying. I look at her with wide eyes. She drags a chair over from another table and sits down. I stand there, completely thrown. Eventually I snap out of it and join Kate at the table.

Carter looks up at Kate with raised brows and she freezes. He frowns and looks at her through narrowed eyes, but then he ignores her behavior and turns back to Gemma. He doesn't even glance at me.

"What is this?" Kate asks. "A double date?"

She sounds angry and her eyes are flashing dangerously. I stare at her and then at Asher. Is she jealous? I've suspected that she's had a crush on Asher for some time now, but this looks like it might be more than a crush. I can't quite figure out what's going on, but the way she glances at Chloe even makes me shrink away. Kate is just like Helen. She doesn't get mad often, but when she does she's goes from 0 to 100 in ten seconds flat.

Asher flinches when Chloe's eyes light up, and she leans into him. Her breasts brush against his arm and he looks away, embarrassed. Kate's anger peaks and I shake my head. If she's trying to keep her crush a secret, then she isn't doing a very good job. At this rate, she definitely won't be able to keep it from Carter, which I'm sure she's been trying to.

Or maybe she can. I glance at Carter, but he hasn't taken his eyes off Gemma once. My heart aches when he smiles at her. She leans into him and whispers into his ear, and he grins roguishly. I don't even want to imagine what she said to him.

I take a bite of my food, but it tastes like cardboard. I sigh and push it away. I'm not hungry anyway. Gemma finally looks at me, as though she only just noticed I was there. She smiles at me sweetly.

"Ah, you're Emilia, right? The pranks you and Carter pull on each other are hilarious. I'm always anxiously awaiting what you two will do next. You seem really close," she says. Her smile wavers at those last words, as though she's wondering just how close we are.

Carter shrugs and answers the unspoken question. "We're not that close. She's just my little sister's nuisance of a best friend. Do you really think we'd be doing the shit we do if we even remotely liked each other?"

I stare at him with wide eyes. What? We're *not close*? I don't think we could've gotten any closer last weekend. And I'm a nuisance?

I bite down on my lip harshly to keep my emotions in check and look down at my tray. Even when our little war was at its height, I always considered us to be friends. Did he always see me as Kate's friend instead of his own?

I try my best to smile at Gemma and nod. "Yeah, he's right. We're not that close. I'm just his sister's bestie. You two look cute together, by the way."

She looks relieved and smiles up at Carter with glowing eyes, but he's looking at me. He looks dismayed to hear me confirm his words.

I smile politely at them and rise. "Excuse me, I'm not really hungry and I have some homework to finish anyway," I say. I grab my bag and rush away, barely able to keep my tears at bay. Kate is so wrapped up in Asher that she doesn't even notice me leave.

Chapter Twenty-One

CARTER

I walk in after an extra long training session to find Kate and Emilia on the sofa, watching some chick flick. Emilia looks up and her breath catches. She stares at my body with longing and then drags her eyes away, her expression clouding. She's mad at me, and she has every right to be. I've spent all day pushing her away, and it seems I've accomplished what I set out to do. So why do I feel so bad?

I drop onto the sofa next to Emilia in my usual seat. I want to be mad at her for ending things before giving us a chance, but I can't stay away from her either. I can't even play hard to get for a whole damn day.

Emilia tries her best to focus on the chick flick she's watching, but she keeps glancing at me. I don't think she even realizes she's doing it, because she keeps catching herself and forcing her eyes back to the screen. It's endearing as hell. I want to talk to her, but I don't know what to say, especially with Kate sitting right next to her. I'm scared I pushed her too far away with the way I acted with Gemma today. I was so intent on creating distance between us, but after just a single day I've already had enough of it. I miss her. I miss seeing her smile and I miss talking to her. It was really tough to have her so close to me and not speak to her, to let Gemma fawn over me instead. I'm worried I really hurt her when I said that we aren't close.

I'm still thinking about what to say when my phone buzzes. I grab it from my pocket and unlock it without thinking. I stare in shock at the message Gemma sent me and blink in disbelief. I only snap out of it when Emilia gasps. She looks at the photo of Gemma's breasts with wide eyes. Her shock makes way for pure agony, and I click the photo away as quickly as I can. Her eyes stay on my phone and she blinks rapidly, as though she's trying to blink away tears. She sniffs and gets up.

"I totally forgot to do Mr. Johnson's homework," she tells Kate, her voice trembling. "I gotta go."

She walks away and just as she turns, I see a single tear fall down her cheek. *Fuck.* Emilia rushes away and slams the door behind her.

Kate frowns. "I thought she already did that. I guess she hasn't finished it yet," she says, focusing her attention back on the movie.

I run a hand through my hair. I was mad when she said we should forget what happened between us. I wanted to show her exactly what it'd be like if I did just that, but *fuck.* I never meant to hurt her, not like this. I don't want her crying over me.

I get up and sneak out the house unnoticed. I walk up to Emilia's house and fish around for her spare keys. I've told her multiple times not to leave it under the plant pot and to pick a safer spot for it, but thankfully she hasn't done that yet. The house is quiet when I walk in, and suddenly I'm worried she isn't even here. I walk to her bedroom and pause just outside of it. I can hear her crying right through the door. She sounds like she's fucking devastated.

I open her door and she looks up when I walk in. She looks hurt and mad as hell. She grabs the first thing she can get hold of and throws it at me, but I catch the little glass globe easily and put it back on her nightstand. She sniffs and rises to her feet, pushing against me with all her strength.

"Get lost, Carter! How dare you come into my house without my permission? You'd better get lost right now," she shouts, her voice wobbly. I sigh and throw my arms around her while she punches against my chest with her tiny little fists. She's furious and hurting, and I hate that I did this to her. "Fuck off," she tells me, sniffing. "I fucking hate you," she shouts, before a sob escapes her lips.

I stand there, unsure what to do. I don't know whether I should go, if I should console her, or if I should kiss her. In the end, I decide on the latter. I thread my hand through her hair and tilt her head up gently. My lips come crashing down on hers and she kisses me back. I lift her into my arms and she wraps her legs around me. I place her on top of her desk and push my hips flush against hers. Her skirt bunches around her waist and she moans when my dick presses against her.

"I hate you," she whispers, biting down on my lip. "I fucking hate you."

I groan and kiss her harder. "I know, baby. I was wrong. I'm sorry," I whisper in between kisses. Emilia grabs my t-shirt and lifts it up. I pull away from her and let her take it off. She's breathing hard and looks at me like she's drunk on lust.

Her eyes suddenly clear, and she glares at me. She looks away and wraps her arms around herself. Her sudden change in attitude throws me off and I straighten awkwardly. Her expression turns sad and I sigh.

"I'm sorry," she says, sounding tortured. "I shouldn't have kissed you back. You're with Gemma, right? Seems like you've been with her for some time. I overheard her saying you took her to some coffee shop a few weeks ago. It's not right for us to do this."

I inhale deeply and shake my head. "Baby, no. I swear I'm not seeing her at all. Hell, I don't even talk to her much. I was mad today, Minx. I was mad at you for pushing me away after the weekend we had. I wasn't thinking straight and I just wanted to make you jealous. I went overboard. I never meant to hurt you, Emilia. I have no idea what Gemma was thinking sending me a photo like that. I guess the little bit of attention I gave her today gave her the wrong idea."

I can tell Emilia doesn't believe me, but she wants to. She looks away and I grab her chin to make her face me. "Look at me, baby. I swear to you, nothing is going on with Gemma. I've never touched her the way I've touched you."

I place my hand on my heart to show her I'm dead serious, and her expression flickers. She looks at me with a small amount of hope and my heart races. I need her to believe me. I don't know why this matters to me so much, but I need her to know there's no one but her.

"Did you kiss her?" she asks, her voice breaking.

I shake my head. "No, Emilia. I swear."

She nods and drops her forehead to my chest. I put my chin on top of her head and hug her tightly.

"No more tears, Minx. Please," I whisper, wiping away the last ones. She nods and shifts to get me closer. She hooks her leg around mine and threads her hands through my hair.

"Carter, it really fucking hurt. The way you ignored me today, seeing you with Gemma, my heart can't take it."

I drop my forehead to hers and close my eyes, inhaling deeply. "Minx, I'm so sorry. When you said you didn't want to be with me, and to forget what happened between us... I get hurt too. You broke my fucking heart. Do you have any idea how long I've wanted you? Then it finally happened and you just walk away so easily, like it was nothing."

Another tear rolls down her cheek and I catch it with my thumb. I hate that she's hurting. I hate that we're in this situation at all.

"I'm sorry, Carter. God, I want to be with you so badly. How could you even think that walking away is easy for me? I want you with my heart and soul. You're all I can think of, Carter. I even dream about you."

"Then why? Why won't you be with me? Why would you ask me to forget it even happened?"

She sniffs and drops her forehead to my shoulder, effectively hiding her face from me. "You know why. You know Kate would lose it if we got together. Lately my friendship with her has been strained enough as it is, thanks to Gabby. She'd never forgive me if she found out we got together."

She wraps her arms around my waist and hugs me tightly, as though she doesn't want to let me go, but she knows she must. I sigh and rest my chin on top of her head. I don't want to hurt Kate either, but I can't see myself staying away from Emilia.

"Carter, I'm serious. We can't."

I run my hand over her hair and then cup the back of her neck. "I know," I whisper. "But I want you, Emilia."

She leans back and looks at me with a sorrowful expression. "No more, okay? Kate would never accept it. I see your family as my own, and I don't want to do anything to jeopardize things. I can't stab them in the back."

I huff in annoyance. "So, what do you want to do, Minx?" I can't blame her for picking her friendship with my sister over me because I've always admired her loyalty, but it still fucking hurts. Emilia looks torn.

"I don't know... maybe we can just be friends?"

I pull away from her and turn my back to her. I stare up at her ceiling, feeling lost. I know she wants me just as much as I want her, yet we still can't be together.

"We can try, Minx. If that's what you really want."

She nods, and that's that.

Chapter Twenty-Two

EMILIA

My phone rings just as I walk into the Clarke's house after school. I glance at it warily before picking up, only to hear someone roar at me, *again*. I have no idea what's happening, but all day people have been calling me only to roar into the phone and hang up.

Carter looks up when I walk into the living room and bursts out laughing when he finds me staring at my phone in disbelief. I look at him through narrowed eyes and glare at him when he takes his phone out of his pocket to take a photo of me.

"You," I say through gritted teeth. "It's you! Why have weird people been calling me all day?"

Carter laughs, and my heart flutters a little. It's one of those loud, deep and uninhibited laughs that totally transform his face. My lips tug up at the edges as he rises from his seat and walks up to me. Just watching Carter laugh like that makes the butterflies in my stomach go wild. I can't even stay annoyed at him.

He pauses in front of me and I can't help but check him out. He's wearing a tight black tee that showcases his muscles spectacularly, and I long to be closer to him. It's been so long since I was last in his arms. Ever since I told Carter that I just wanted to be friends, we've stayed away from each other. We've been dancing around each other, toeing the line of friendship, both of us fighting our desire and our feelings.

Carter stands a little too close to me and wraps his hand around my waist. He leans into me and I place my hands on his chest, my palms flat against his pecs. I'm dying to run my hands over his body and to feel him tense underneath my touch.

"Have people been calling you and doing this?" he says, right before roaring loudly, right into my ear. I push against him and he bursts out laughing again.

"What did you do?" I say, shaking my head. Just seeing him so pleased with himself makes my annoyance melt away.

He bites down on his lip cheekily and my mind wanders back to when he lifted me onto my desk and kissed me all those weeks ago. His eyes darken and his gaze drops to my lips. He inhales deeply and closes his eyes before looking away. Is he thinking about that kiss too?

"Yes, that. Why have people calling me and doing *that*?" I say, my voice far more husky than I meant it to be. Carter grins and my heart skips a beat.

"I printed out fifty pages of an ad that promises a lucky winner a hundred dollars for the best Chewbacca impression. I stuck them all around town and put your phone number on it with instructions that said to call you, do the impression and then hang up. I wrote on it that we'd call back the winner and that we'd disqualify any phone call that lasted more than four seconds."

I close my eyes and try my best not to burst out laughing. It's funny as hell — I've gotta give him that. Annoying, but funny.

I hear Kate's laughter behind us and I take a step away from Carter, my heart filling with unease and guilt.

"You *didn't*," she says. She walks up to us and high fives Carter, earning herself a glare from me.

"Kate, you're supposed to be on my team," I whine. She laughs and wraps her arm around my shoulder.

"I am, Milly, but this one is really funny. Don't worry though, I'll help you get back at him."

She winks at me, and I smile back. I love it when Kate helps me pull pranks on Carter. When we join hands against him, the pranks are always extra epic. Kate smiles as though she already has something in mind.

She grabs my hand and pulls me up the stairs. "Okay, I have the *best* idea," she tells me, a wicked grin on her face. I laugh and follow her into her room — I can't freaking wait. Kate walks to her desk and googles images of large bugs before picking one randomly. She prints it out and gives it to me to cut out. It looks gross and I shudder .

"What exactly are we doing with this?" I ask with raised brows. Kate grins and tips her head towards the door.

"Come on, you'll see. This is going to be awesome. It's so simple, but it's going to be fantastic."

I follow her into Carter's room, both of us on our tiptoes. We try to be quiet, but our constant giggles totally defeat the purpose. Kate takes the cutout from me and then sticks it on the inside of Carter's bedside lamp. She then turns it on and I gasp. It actually looks as though there's some large disgusting bug inside the lamp. She turns it back off and I smirk.

"You evil genius," I say, shaking my head. She looks smug and holds her hand up. I high five her and laugh all the way back to her room. Carter is going to be freaking terrified.

"Milly?" Helen shouts. I pause and stick my head into the hallway. "Milly?" she shouts again. I rush down the stairs with Kate on my heels. Helen is in the kitchen and has a bunch of baking supplies spread out on the counter.

"I want to make apple pie, could you help me, honey?" she says. I nod and walk to the sink to wash my hands. Kate stands in the kitchen, frozen, her jaw locked.

"Why didn't you ask me to help too, Mom?" she asks.

Helen pauses and looks at Kate in surprise. "Oh sweetie, I'd love for you to help, but you hate baking."

Kate clenches her jaw and looks at me angrily. Even though I haven't done anything, I feel horrible.

"You still could've asked," she says to Helen. Kate walks towards me and washes her hands so roughly that she splashes water all over the counter. I'm suddenly tense and on edge, even though I know I didn't do anything wrong.

I get to work as Helen gives Kate some instructions. We've made this pie so many times that I can do it in my sleep. I pretty much work on auto-pilot, and Helen and I move in sync. She adds small amounts of butter while I use two forks to work it through the dry ingredients. We learned long ago that the mixture gets too warm if we use our hands.

Kate slams the apples down on the counter and glares at both Helen and me. "Looks like you don't even need or want my help."

I shake my head just like Helen does, but Kate's expression tells me nothing we say will placate her now. Lately her temper has been a bit weird and I'm not sure what to make of it.

She grabs her phone from the counter and turns towards the door. "I'm going to Gabby's house," she tells us. I drop the forks and wipe my hands on my skirt.

"Kate, no, please. Just stay and help us. It'll be so much fun," I tell her, my tone pleading. Kate shakes her head and looks from me to her mother.

"Nope, thanks. You two have fun," she says, her eyes flashing with bitterness. I don't know what to do — should I follow her or should I let her go? I move to chase her, but Helen grabs my hand and shakes her head.

"I'll talk to her, Milly. Just let her be for now. You know as well as I do you won't be able to talk any sense into her when she's mad."

I nod and take the fork she's handing me. My heart is in agony. It feels like my friendship with Kate keeps getting worse and I can't figure out what I'm doing wrong. I don't want to lose her, and I have no idea how to hold on to her when she pushes me away so vehemently. She's been hanging out with Gabby more and more often, and the more time she spends with her, the more she seems to resent me. The distance between us seems to increase every day, and I'm terrified she'll soon be out of reach.

Chapter Twenty-Three

Emilia

I walk into the Clarke's house and sigh inwardly. Gabby and Kate are both sitting at the dining table with Kate. These days Gabby is here more often than not, and she usually makes me feel like the odd one out. The two of them look up when I walk in, and Gabby looks particularly disappointed to see me. It's obvious that she was expecting Carter instead.

Helen smiles when she spots me and waves me over. I join her in the kitchen and wash my hands before helping her with dinner.

"How was school, sweetie?" she asks.

"It was good."

My grades are the same, but everything feels different lately. More often than not Kate is ditching me for Gabby and I've started to feel lonely at school. Thankfully, Carter keeps a good eye on me and hangs out with me every once in a while. We've been careful to stay within the boundaries of friendship, but it's not easy. Every time we're alone, he looks at me like he *wants* me.

"Kate's grades seem to have dropped a little. You guys don't study together anymore?" Helen asks. I shake my head. We used to have short study sessions every day to keep each other on track, but she's been skipping those recently. Helen sighs. She looks worried, and I wish I could make her feel better.

"I'll remind her to study with me," I say, knowing that my words will fall on deaf ears. Helen smiles gratefully and sighs.

My phone buzzes and I fish it out of my pocket. I bite back a smile when I see that it's Carter. He's convinced me to let him hide out in my house in order to avoid Gabby. She's at the Clarke's almost every day now and takes every single opportunity to hang around. Carter studying at my house was meant to be a one-time thing that has somehow lasted for weeks now. I was hesitant at first, but when I realized how persistent Gabby is, I gave in. Besides, most of the time I'm not even with him, so it doesn't really matter that much.

Devil: *Can you bring me my AP Chemistry book? I forgot to bring it.*

Emilia: *Where are you?*

I don't know why I even bother asking. I know exactly where he is.

Devil: *In your bedroom. I locked my door before I left but you've got a key, right?*

I chuckle to myself. A couple of years ago Helen put locks on all the bedroom doors to prevent Carter and me from pulling pranks on each other. I copied his bedroom key within weeks, and he always knew, but he never bothered to change the lock. Guess it's finally coming in handy for him now.

Emilia: *I don't get why you can't just study in your own bedroom and just lock the door. Or, you know, study at my dining table?*

Devil: *Last time I studied in my bedroom that viper kept bothering me. Do you really think a locked door will stop her? Besides, I like your bedroom. It's cozy.*

Cozy? Seriously? I roll my eyes and sigh. He keeps making a mess of my desk and my bed. The coziness he's referring to is really just his mess. There are notes scattered all over my bedroom.

At least he helps me look over my homework and helps me study for my own tests. Thanks to Carter, I've been acing my essays with ease.

Devil: *Can you bring snacks too? I want the Cheez-Its.*

Devil: *Please.*

Emilia: *I can't believe you eat that over-processed crap. I'm not bringing that for you. How about an apple?*

I smile to myself and grab the Cheez-Its from the cupboard. I can't stand them, but Carter adores them. I throw a few packets into my bag without thinking and look up to find Helen looking at me, baffled.

"I... I was just thinking... I just thought they'd be nice to study with?"

Helen blinks and nods slowly, as though she doesn't believe me for a second. She then grabs a bag of Cheetos and hands me that too. I stare at it in dismay, and I'm about to decline when my phone lights up again.

Devil: *I want Cheetos too. I think mom bought some the other day. Can you bring them?*

I stare at the text in disbelief and Helen laughs. "Cheetos are good for studying too," she says. I nod and put the Cheetos in my bag.

"You two coming in for dinner later?" she asks. I stare at the lasagna she's making longingly and nod. She purses her lips and looks away. "Just so you know, Gabby is having dinner with us. I'll drop by your house later with some snacks too, but the Cheetos and the Cheez-Its will do for now."

She knows Carter has been hiding out in my house, but she's been helping me keep it from Kate and Gabby nonetheless. She usually doesn't like it when we're left unattended, but this time she's letting it slide. I guess because Carter was genuinely struggling to study at home, and it's almost impossible to make Kate understand how disruptive Gabby's behavior is. Both Carter and Helen have tried to speak to her about it, but her reply is usually the same. In her opinion, Gabby should be allowed to come over if I am. And if I'm allowed to pull pranks on Carter, then Gabby is allowed to annoy him a little too. I almost feel guilty for the role I've unwittingly played in this situation. I know Helen feels a little helpless. She doesn't want to have double standards, and I get that.

I have to walk past Kate and Gabby to go up the stairs to Carter's room, and I cringe when Kate's voice stops me. I feel like I'm doing something wrong, and I just know that if they find out Carter is at my house, Kate is going to misunderstand and Gabby is going to want to come over.

"Milly, what're you doing here?" Kate asks. The question surprises me a little. I can't remember a single time in the last couple of years that she's asked me that question. I often come over randomly and she's never said anything before. I smile at Kate and shake my head.

"I think I left my history textbook in your room. Can't find it anywhere," I lie. The lies come easier to me now, and I hate it. I hate how easy it has become to find an excuse not to spend time with her.

Gabby rolls her eyes. "God, you're such a nerd. Do you *ever* do anything fun?" she asks.

I roll my eyes. She needs to have less fun and do more studying, but that's not my problem. Kate laughs and it hits me right in the heart. It feels like she's ganging up on me with Gabby and it hurts.

"When is Carter coming home?" Gabby asks. "I haven't seen him all week. Are you sure he's gonna be home for dinner?"

I frown at Kate and she looks away. I raise my brows when she smiles at Gabby. "Yeah, my brother loves food more than anything. He wouldn't miss dinner for the world."

Gabby huffs and crosses her arms. "You also said he spends most of his time either at football practice or in his bedroom studying, but he hasn't been coming home until really late for days now. Do you think he might be studying at the library? We should go there tomorrow."

I shake my head "What does it matter what Carter does or where he is? You're here to hang out with Kate, aren't you?"

I don't get what's going on with Kate. It's so obvious that Gabby is only befriending her because she wants to get close to Carter. Why is Kate allowing it? Is it just because Gabby is the most popular girl in school? Kate never used to care about stuff like that.

Kate looks at me pleadingly, her expression so sad that my heart breaks. I bite down on my lip and decide to shut up. I shake my head and walk up the stairs silently.

Carter waves at me from my bedroom when I walk in and I freeze. He's standing right beside my window, and I always thought that particular spot was out of sight from his room. It really *isn't*. I can see him standing there clearly. How did I not realize this? Does that mean he might have noticed me ogling him? How freaking embarrassing. I guess I got lucky and he just didn't notice, because there's no way he'd ever let that go.

I'm flustered as hell as I make my way back home. My heart hammers in my chest as I walk up the stairs. Surely he didn't realize. There's no way Carter knows I've been looking into his room. He'd have teased me about it, wouldn't he? My cheeks are bright red when I walk into my bedroom. Carter looks up at me in surprise and I stare down at my feet, beyond embarrassed. I clear my throat awkwardly and put his snacks and his textbook on my desk.

"Hey, what's wrong?" he asks. My eyes involuntarily move back to my window and my cheeks heat up even more. I shake my head and look away. I can't even look at him, I'm that embarrassed. How freaking awkward. Carter chuckles and I look up at him. Surely he doesn't realize what I'm so distressed about?

He smiles at me sweetly and pulls me closer to him. He spreads his legs and leans back on my desk chair so I can stand closer. "What's wrong?" he asks. I shake my head and stare at his shoulder. I was so shameless when I was peeping, but now that there's a chance I might've gotten caught, I'm suddenly ashamed.

Carter grins and pulls me closer. He rests his chin on top of my shoulder and I melt into him. He gives the best hugs and I love the way he feels against me.

We've done so well at keeping things appropriate between us, and I guess our little hugs toe the line, but I don't think I could do without them. Carter sighs and holds me just a little tighter before pulling away. I take a step back when all I really want to do is throw myself in his arms.

"I looked at your calculus homework and it's a freaking mess," he tells me. "Look," he points to my homework. He's marked every error with a pencil, and he's written down the correct calculations.

"You don't have to do that for me, you know," I say, my heart fluttering. He's so thoughtful. He's crazy busy with his own homework, tests, and football practice. He's so tired lately that I've caught him fast asleep with his head on my desk multiple times now. Despite that, he still took the time to help me with my own homework. Why is he so amazing? I almost wish he wasn't so kind to me, so I might actually be able to get over him.

Carter shakes his head and smiles. "It's the least I can do considering I've pretty much taken over your bedroom."

He starts to walk me through the calculations and I try to focus on his words as best as I can, but I'm struggling. I want him. I hate having him so close to me and having to resist.

Carter suddenly freezes and then jumps up. He grabs my shoulders and tackles me to the floor. I brace for the inevitable pain I'm about to feel, but Carter hugs me and turns us around so he falls onto his back with me on top of him. He grunts when he hits the floor and wraps his hands around my head protectively.

"What the hell?" I shout. Carter looks at me with wide eyes and sits up slightly.

"You left my bedroom door unlocked," he whispers. I frown and rise to my knees so I can peek into his room the way he's doing.

I gasp when I see Gabby standing in the middle of his room.

She looks around curiously and then walks up to the window. She stares straight into my room and we both hide. Carter pulls me back to the floor and I giggle at his horrified expression.

"I can't believe she's in my fucking room," he whispers, shuddering, and I burst out laughing. Carter wraps his hand over my mouth and turns us over so I'm lying underneath him.

"You little Minx. Please tell me you didn't do it on purpose," he whispers. I shake my head, but I can't stop laughing. He looks so horrified.

"You realize she can't hear you, right? You don't have to whisper. You know, I bet she's rolling around in your sheets. I wonder if she thinks she can just spread her scent all over your bed and mark it as hers?"

Carter looks terrified and I laugh even harder.

"Not funny, Minx," he says. Carter rolls on top of me and pushes my hands above my head. The mood changes instantly and my eyes fall to his lips. I want him. I want him so badly and I know he wants me too.

Carter leans in and his lips brush over mine. I sigh and tilt my head a little, giving him easier access to my lips. I know we shouldn't do this, but I can't help myself. Staying away from him gets harder every day.

Carter is about to kiss me when the slamming of my front door interrupts us. We're both startled and jump up and away from each other.

"That's probably your mom," I whisper. "She said she'd drop by with some snacks for us."

Carter runs a hand through his hair and nods before walking out of my room. I follow him down, feeling as frustrated as I know he is.

Chapter Twenty-Four

CARTER

"Ugh, I'm starving," I shout as I walk into my house. Emilia walks into the hallway and smiles at me.

"Hey, you're home," she says. My heart starts racing. She looks cute as hell with her apron on and a smudge of flour on her cheek. She walks up to me and I pause in front of her.

She gently tugs on my hands, and I blink. I didn't even realize I'd been rubbing my shoulders — they've been aching all day. Guess I've been pushing myself a bit too hard lately. Her hands replace mine and she stands on her tiptoes as she massages my shoulders, her expression serious. I stare down at her and smile.

I cup her cheek gently and wipe away the flour. She looks up at me and smiles so sweetly that my heart fills to the brim with tenderness. A simple smile from her makes me forget how shit my day was. My hands move to her waist and I wrap my hands around her. Her waist is so tiny than I can wrap my hands around her almost entirely. I fucking love it.

"Long day?" she asks. I nod and sigh as she works on one of my knots. A small moan escapes my lips and Emilia looks up at me with flushed cheeks. I grin at her and she bites down on her lip. I take a step closer to her until her body is flush against mine.

"How was your day, Minx? I barely saw you today."

She's been hanging out with Kate at school, and I've been avoiding Kate and Gabby like the plague. It's gotten so ridiculous that I'm contemplating spending time with them just so I can have a few moments with my Minx. Our schedules keep clashing. We haven't even been able to study together.

"It was good," she replies, but her expression falls slightly. I know her day wasn't *good*. It never is when she's around Gabby, yet she keeps suffering through it for Kate. I don't understand why she does this to herself. Her arms move around my neck and she closes the distance between us while my arms wrap tighter. She leans into my embrace and inhales deeply while I hug her. Hugs with Emilia are just the best. It's one of those little things that always makes my day, no matter how shit it's been. It seems like it's the same for her.

"Oh, you're home," my mother says. Emilia jumps away from me and I stiffen. My mom is standing in the hallway and looks at us through narrowed eyes. I smile at my mom and she purses her lips. "Emilia has been helping me make chicken Kiev. I'm pretty excited about what it'll end up tasting like. Looks good, anyway," she tells me. I nod and follow her into the kitchen, grateful that she didn't say anything about us hugging in the hallway.

I lean back against the counter as Emilia preps what looks like cauliflower mash. My stomach grumbles loudly and she laughs. I glare at her half-heartedly and watch as she finishes up dinner with my mom. A strand of her hair falls in front of her face and I gently tuck it behind her ear.

"How'd you end up doing on your calculus test?" I ask. "You said you'd text me, but you didn't."

Her expression falls and I sigh. I figured she didn't do that well on it when she didn't text me her results, but I was hoping I was wrong. She pouts and focuses on her mash instead.

"I'll tutor you, all right? It's really not that hard. Don't worry about it, Minx."

She nods, but she looks worried. Emilia has always hated not being good at something academically. She's one of the few people I know that has always had her heart set on getting a scholarship, even more so since her dad told her that her mother took away her college fund. I know continuously failing calculus worries her.

I cup her cheek and make her face me. "It'll be fine. I promise, Minx."

She nods and smiles up at me, setting my heart at ease. Whenever she's near me, I get so absorbed in her I forget anyone else is around. My mother clears her throat and we both stiffen. Seems like I'm not the only one who forgot about her, because Emilia looks up at me with wide eyes. I smile and pull away from her.

"Kate just texted to ask if Gabby can stay for dinner," she says. Emilia and I both look at my mother in dismay and she laughs.

"Just say no," I tell her. Mom shakes her head.

"Too late. They're already on their way — should be here soon."

I groan and move to escape, but my mom grabs my elbow. "No, you don't," she tells me. "I've barely seen you recently. You're staying for dinner."

Emilia chuckles, but my mom levels her with a stare. "You're staying too, young lady."

Emilia's expression falls and I burst out laughing. My amusement is short-lived because the front door opens and Kate and Gabby walk in.

Gabby's eyes light up when she sees me, and I cringe subconsciously while Emilia tenses.

"Oh hi, Carter!" she says. She practically skips towards me and throws herself against me before I can step away. She hugs me tightly while my arms lie against my sides. It's awkward as hell.

I glance at Emilia. She's gritting her teeth as she looks away. I sigh helplessly. I didn't even do anything. I grab Gabby's shoulders and forcefully remove her when she's still hugging me ten seconds later. The girl has no shame at all.

"I'm so glad you're here," she tells me. She hooks her arm around mine and tries to drag me towards the dining room. I glance at Kate, but she sends me a pleading stare that I struggle to resist. What the hell am I supposed to do here? Emilia looks more and more annoyed with every second that goes by, while Kate looks happier with every second that I let Gabby cling to me.

"Uh, yeah. It's good to see you too, Layla. Or is it Chloe? I can't remember."

Gabby freezes, and she looks up at me in disbelief while Kate throws me a look that would've killed me outright if it could. Gabby's expression falls and it's almost like watching a mask crack. For a second her inner harpy emerges, but she reins it in quickly.

"It's Gabby, actually. I'm your sister's best friend," she tells me. I pull my arm out of her grip and place my palm on Emilia's lower back.

"No, you're not. *Emilia* is my sister's best friend." I glance at Emilia, my eyes running over her body on purpose before I glance back at Gabby. "And you, *Abby*, are not Emilia."

She glares at Emilia, who I can tell is biting back a smile, and then looks up at me. "It's *Gabby*," she says. I shrug and walk past them. I'm tempted to pull Emilia along with me, but I know she wouldn't like it if I did that.

"He's such a dick," I hear Gabby say, and I smile victoriously. Mission accomplished. "But that just makes him hotter," she adds. Wait, *what*? What is wrong with this girl? How the hell does her brain work?

My mother laughs at my expression and shakes her head. She winks at me and I sigh inwardly. I just know this dinner is going to be hellish. At least Emilia will be there and I won't have to suffer alone.

Chapter Twenty-Five

EMILIA

Carter sets the table while Helen and I finish up dinner. I try my best not to think of how Gabby must be clinging onto Carter by now. Just seeing her hug him annoyed me. I can't stand her.

"Try this," I say to Helen as I hold up a spoon for her.

She takes a bite of the chicken Kiev and grins. "Turned out great, didn't it?"

I nod and smile. I love it when we try new recipes or when Helen teaches me to make a new dish. It's our way of bonding, and lately we haven't done enough of it. Kate has been pushing me away and I haven't been coming over every single day like I used to. She's been making me feel like I'm intruding, and I'm worried I might actually have been. I never meant to, but I guess I got a bit too comfortable here. I overstepped.

Helen takes a bite of the cauliflower mash and sighs in delight. "This is amazing, Milly. I love this. We should definitely make mash more often."

Carter walks into the kitchen with a stormy expression and looks at us. "Just shoot me now," he says.

Helen and I both burst out laughing. Carter shakes his head and walks towards me. "Minx, I'm not joking. If she looks at me with those wide bug-like creepy eyes one more time, I might actually cry. I'm *terrified*."

His arms slip around my waist, and he pulls me closer. I look up at him and giggle as I shake my head. Helen clears her throat and Carter steps away from me, startled. It's like neither one of us realizes when we touch anymore.

"You two... I've ignored this for as long as I could, but I have to ask. Are you dating?"

My heart stops, and Carter looks as shocked as I do. My cheeks turn bright crimson and I shake my head. "I — no... we aren't."

Carter crosses his arms and stares at his mother thoughtfully. "What if we were?"

Helen sighs and leans back against the kitchen counter. "I love both of you kids, but you're just that. You're kids. I know I'm not your mother, Emilia, but we had an agreement that there would be no dating until you turn sixteen, which is still a couple of weeks from now."

I nod and look down at my feet, wishing the floor would open up and swallow me whole. I'm so embarrassed.

"So it's fine as soon as she turns sixteen?"

I look up at Carter with wide eyes and shake my head to tell him to knock it off, but he ignores me.

Helen sighs and pinches the bridge of her nose. "I'm sorry, Carter, but I don't think it'd be a good idea for you two to date. For one, you're far too young. I wouldn't be opposed to it once you're a couple of years older, but *not* now. And then there's your sister. I think you know how she feels about the idea of you dating Emilia. What do you think it would do to her? You'll be going off to college in a few months, but Emilia and Kate will still be here. Their friendship won't ever be the same again because Kate will never get over it. She'll view it as a betrayal, no matter how you try to explain. Besides, you're teenagers. I'm sure you think your relationship could survive while you're so far away from each other, but long-distance relationships are incredibly hard. I don't think it's a good idea for you to be in any relationship at all, at least during your first year of college."

I bite down on my lip harshly and nod. She's right, of course. I knew she'd feel this way, but I'm still upset. It still hurts to know that even Helen thinks Carter and I shouldn't be together. I hate knowing that I'd be letting her down if I followed my heart. She's the only mother figure I've got in my life, and the idea of her being disappointed in me breaks my heart.

Helen cups my cheek and sighs. "Milly, I love you as my own daughter. I always have. I'm not saying I don't want you and Carter to ever get together, okay? Just not now. Not while you're still so young and have so much of your lives left to live."

I nod and try my best to keep my tears at bay. I'm not even sure why I'm suddenly so upset. Carter and I already decided to stay away from each other anyway. It's not like we're dating and she's asking us to break up, yet it feels that way. Carter looks as upset as I am and runs a hand through his hair, messing it up.

Kate walks into the kitchen and freezes, her eyes moving between us as she takes in the tense atmosphere. Helen smiles at her and hands her a serving dish. "Let's go have dinner, kids."

Carter and I are both quiet as we sit down, both of us lost in thought.

"So Carter, what college are you planning on going to?" Gabby asks. Carter looks up at her dazedly, his response delayed.

"USC," he replies. My heart sinks from the reminder. Carter will soon be gone and I'm not sure I can handle that. The idea that he's leaving terrifies me. He'll forget about me and move on with his life soon. He'll be at college and he'll be moving on to bigger and better things while I'll still be stuck here in Woodstock. I have no doubt that he'll make it to USC in LA. Soon he'll be so far out of reach that I'll be lucky if we even remain friends.

"Oh, my cousin goes there. I might go see her and we can hang out then. How fun would that be?" Gabby says. Carter doesn't respond and Kate glares at him, but he doesn't even seem to notice, he's as lost in his thoughts as I am.

Gabby focuses her attention on me and smiles. "It's kind of surprising that you're always here, Emilia. Kate and you didn't even hang out today. Do you have dinner here every day? That's so weird. Don't you have your own family? Doesn't your mom make you dinner?"

I freeze, my heart twisting painfully at the memory of my mom. The older I get, the harder it becomes to remember her. I haven't tried to get in touch with her since my dad told me she accused me of stalking her. She walked out of my life and I was a fool to hang onto her when she chose to leave me. I'll never, ever do that again. I'll never cling to someone who leaves me.

I look down at my plate, unsure of what to say. Kate didn't invite me to dinner, and I'm still here. I'm old enough to make my own dinner now, so I should probably stop coming over every day.

"Oh wait, you don't have a mother, do you?" Gabby says.

William straightens and looks at Gabby furiously. "That's enough. I won't have you insulting or hurting Emilia in my house. You either apologize or leave," he tells Gabby.

I'm shocked and really touched. William is a man of very few words and usually leaves Helen to solve issues however she sees fit. I can count the amount of times he's scolded one of us on one hand. Even Kate looks surprised to hear her father speak up. She nods in agreement, but her expression clouds over when Carter speaks up.

"Leave," he tells Gabby. "I'm done putting up with you. You're no longer welcome in my house. If you want to hang out with Kate, you can do so at school or elsewhere, but not here."

Kate frowns. "That's a bit harsh. Gabby isn't wrong, is she? Why the hell would you ban her from the house when she's done nothing wrong? All because Emilia can't handle the truth?"

Carter looks at her in disbelief. "I can't even recognize you anymore, Kate. Take a good look in the mirror and see if you can look yourself in the eye after the words you just spoke. I've never been more disappointed in you."

Kate gulps, and her eyes fill with pain. I hate that I'm at the center of this conflict and that there's nothing I can do about it. Kate gets up with such force that her chair topples over. She looks at Carter with tears in her eyes and storms off. Gabby jumps up to follow her and glares at Carter and me before walking away.

"Kate! Stop right there," Helen shouts. Kate glances back at her mother and then turns away and walks out. Helen jumps up and follows her while Carter grabs my hand.

"Kate hasn't been herself recently, Minx. Don't worry about it, okay? You're always welcome here," he says.

I nod, but I know it isn't true.

Chapter Twenty-Six

EMILIA

My doorbell rings and I frown. Carter is still at football practice and won't be home for the next couple of hours, and Kate is meant to be at the shopping center with Gabby. I drop my pencil and make my way down.

I'm surprised to find Kate at my doorstep, and I'm not even remotely happy to see her. These days she only spends time with me when Gabby bails on her, and that's happening more and more often since the last dinner we had. Carter stood by his word and refused to let Gabby into the house, and he refuses to be anywhere near her now. I'm not surprised that it hasn't taken Gabby long to stop hanging out with Kate. I don't want to be Kate's second choice. Not anymore. I've always tried my best to put her first — I've always tried to put her happiness above mine, and even above Carter's. I'm done.

"Hey," she says. She storms into my house and plops down on the sofa. I follow her in and sit down next to her quietly. It's somewhat weird to have her here. Carter has really started to feel at home here, but Kate never has. She has always insisted that I come to her house instead, and I've never minded it because it allowed me to spend time with Helen and Carter too.

"Gabby bailed on me when she found out Carter is at football practice," she says. I figured as much. I'm pretty sure Gabby only really used to drag Kate to the shopping center so she had an excuse to get Carter to pick them up. The shopping center is close enough to walk to from school, but far enough from our houses that someone needs to go pick up Kate. The first few times it actually worked, but recently he's been outright refusing to go get them, forcing Helen to go instead.

"That sucks," I murmur, unsure of what else I could say. Every time I tried to warn her that Gabby isn't a real friend, my warnings fell on deaf ears. Every time I spoke up, she'd send me a pleading look requesting me to stop. Kate's been pushing me away in her pursuit of Gabby's friendship. And what for? Popularity?

"I messed up," she says. She buries her head in her hands and breathes in shakily. "I know I did, Milly. I'm sorry. I just..."

She takes a steadying breath and sniffs. My anger melts away and I wrap my arm around her. As soon as I do, a sob escapes her lips, as though she's just been trying to hold it in the entire time. She starts crying and I stroke her shoulder gently. I can't stand seeing Kate in tears and my own heart feels like it's breaking too. I was so intent on staying mad at her, but how can I when she's crying like this?

"I know what you're thinking, Milly, but she didn't approach me because of Carter. She genuinely liked me for me. She didn't even realize that I was Carter's sister until I told her. He always ruins everything for me."

I bite down on my lip to keep from snapping at her. Everyone knows that she's Carter's sister — our town isn't very big. Most of us know each other, and everyone definitely knows Carter. She's deceiving herself if she's pretending Gabby didn't know exactly who she was.

"Kate, everyone knows everyone here," I say. We might not

know each other well, but we all do sort of recognize each other by face. Granted, Gabby is still relatively new here, but she's been living in Woodstock for almost a year now. It's impossible for her not to have known who Kate is. Kate shakes her head and looks up at me through teary eyes.

"No, she really didn't know. She was so surprised, Milly. I wish I never told her. I only told her because I knew she had a bit of a crush on him and I felt bad keeping it from her. She would've found out eventually anyway and you know..."

I shake my head. I *don't* know. I don't understand. Kate rests her head on my shoulder and sniffs, her shoulders shaking.

"She just changed after she found out. She kept wanting to spend time with him, and as her friend I felt bad for not helping her out a little. It didn't really hurt to create some opportunity for her, you know."

My heart aches at the mere thought of Carter with Gabby. What would I have done if Kate's ploys had actually worked, if they actually started dating? I can just imagine her sitting next to him in the car every morning, or seeing them together at the house. My heart twists painfully at the mental image I've conjured, and I grit my teeth.

"I thought you hated it when your friends like Carter. Didn't you stop being friends with Jennifer two years ago because she liked him?"

Kate looks away and nods. "Yeah, and I was right. Just once I thought it'd be okay, that my friendship with Gabby wouldn't necessarily be affected by her liking Carter, but look at me now. I don't even get it. Every single time any of my friends like him, my friendships just fall apart. All they do is use me to try to see him or to get information about him."

She bursts out crying again, this time even harder, and my heart breaks for her. I get how she feels, but I'm also certain that Gabby knew full well who she was when she approached Kate. It was obvious to everyone except her.

"You know what Layla told me? Apparently it all started as a bet. The other girls on our squad dared Gabby to try and get Carter to date her because so far they'd all failed. I think that's why she befriended me, you know. I think I was just part of the plan. I wonder if any single aspect of our friendship was even real."

I wipe away her tears as best as I can and push her hair away from her face. I knew Gabby had an ulterior motive of some sort, but this is even worse than I expected.

"Don't cry, Kate," I say. "I promise it'll be fine. You don't need her anyway. You've got me, babe."

She nods and hugs me tightly as she chokes on her sobs. She can barely even breathe because she's crying so hard. She clings to me as I stroke her back in an effort to calm her down, but nothing seems to work .

"I was so horrible to you, too. Gabby didn't like you because you're so close to my family and Carter, and I stupidly pushed you away to please her. I can't believe I did that to you, Milly. She kept telling me you must be in love with Carter and that you were using me to hang out with him, when all along it was her that felt that way. I should've known you'd never do that to me."

She tries to inhale deeply but fails, and a fresh bout of tears run down her cheeks. "You'd never do that to me, would you?" she asks. I nod reassuringly and wipe her tears away with my thumbs. Seeing her cry this way breaks my heart. I hated who she was around Gabby, but she's still my best friend. She's still the girl I grew up with, the girl I've shared everything with in the last seven years, and that has never hesitated to share everything with me in return, her family included.

"Promise me, Milly. Please, promise me. Promise that you'll never, ever start liking Carter. Don't ever fall for him, please."

Fat teardrops fall from her eyes, and I nod without thinking. I always knew Carter and I could never be together. I always knew it would jeopardize my friendship with Kate. It's the reason I pushed him away after our weekend at the cabin when all I wanted was to pull him closer.

Kate holds up her pinky and grabs my hand to entwine hers with mine. "Pinky promise you'll never ever fall for Carter," she says. I close my eyes and nod while crossing my fingers behind my back. It's far too late for me to be making such a promise solemnly, but I'll do all I can to prevent Kate from ever finding out.

"I promise, Kate," I reply.

She exhales in relief and looks up at me. "You're my best friend, Milly, the only friend that's stuck with me through thick and thin. I don't know what I'd do without you. Thank you for putting me first."

My stomach twists. I feel like I'm stabbing her in the back by keeping silent about what's been going on with Carter, but if I tell her, our friendship will never be the same, if it survives at all.

I nod at her and try my best to smile. "I love you, Kate," I tell her, and I truly mean it. The issue is that I'm pretty sure I love Carter too.

Chapter Twenty-Seven

CARTER

I have no idea why Emilia has been looking so miserable when it's her birthday. Her sixteenth birthday, no less. She's been counting down the days, yet I've barely seen her smile today. Mom and Kate have taken full control of entertaining her today while Emilia's dad, my dad, and I have been tasked with picking up the cake and decorating the house.

"Kate just texted me to say that they'll be back in an hour," I tell John. He nods and claps me on the back. I can barely look him in the eyes these days. I guess sneaking into his house without his knowledge will do that to you. If only that were the only thing I've been doing. I haven't stolen any kisses from Emilia recently, but I've wanted to. I'm pretty sure her dad would murder me if he knew what I've done to his daughter underneath his roof.

My mind instantly flashes back to the day Gemma sent me that god awful photo of her tits that made my Minx cry. That was the last time I kissed her, and had it been up to me, we'd have done much more than that.

"I'm afraid there's been a mix-up," the lady at the cake shop tells us. "I can see you ordered a chocolate cake, but your order note is attached to a strawberry one."

She shows it to us, and indeed, it says *Happy Birthday, Emilia*. My dad and I both groan, but Emilia's dad just shrugs. "It's pretty enough. I'm sure it'll be fine."

I shake my head. "Emilia hates anything that's strawberry flavored," I tell him. I look at the employee that's helping us through narrowed eyes. She looks familiar, but I can't quite place her. One of Gabby's friends? As far as I'm aware, Gabby and Kate have finally stopped being friends. I hate how Kate is all over Emilia now, as though she didn't ditch her the second a more popular girl befriended her. I love my sister, but I hate the way she's been behaving. I can't believe Emilia lets her get away with it so easily too.

"That's nonsense. Emilia loves strawberries. She eats them all the time," John says.

I close my eyes and sigh. "Yeah, she loves strawberries. She just hates anything that's artificially strawberry flavored." She can't stand the fake flavor, but she loves the real thing.

"It's all right, John," my dad says to Emilia's dad. "We can just get a refund on the deposit for this one and get her another one."

I nod in agreement, but Emilia's dad shakes his head. "No, this'll do. I don't want to get her one of those supermarket cakes. I think this'll be fine. She'll like this better than anything else we can get her on such short notice."

He hands over his credit card and I sigh. I can't believe this. I know for a fact that she's going to hate this cake and that she does, in fact, have a thing for the chocolate cake at the small bakery down the road. I wish we hadn't trusted John to pick a cake. It's obvious he doesn't know his daughter at all.

I'm about to interrupt when my father shakes his head at me. He throws me a look that tells me to shut up. It's her sixteenth birthday, for God's sake. She should at least have a cake that she'll love. I know it's not our place, but it's clear even *my* dad knows Emilia better than John does.

I'm stewing as we make our way back to the house. I'll need to find some time to grab her a chocolate cake, because I know she'll hate this one. I'll be very surprised if she even takes a single bite. I've got a surprise planned for her tonight, and I hope everything goes to plan.

We make it back to the house minutes before the girls do. Thankfully, we decorated everything before we went to pick up the cake. All three of us are in a rush to get the final things done, but we just about manage.

I'm oddly excited when the front door opens and Emilia walks in. On cue, all three of us pop our party poppers, sending confetti flying everywhere. Emilia jumps in fright and then smiles when she spots us and the decorations.

"Happy birthday!" we all yell. She giggles and we hug her one by one. I'm delighted when she lingers in my arms for a couple of seconds longer, and I press a covert kiss to her neck.

My mom throws an arm around her shoulder and pulls her towards the living room. We've got dozens of balloons against the ceiling and her birthday cake on the coffee table. She gasps as she looks around, her eyes finding mine. I wink at her and she giggles.

Her dad starts singing happy birthday while my mom lights the candles. Emilia falls to her knees in front of the coffee table and stares up at all of us, her face lit up with pure delight. I'm relieved to see her enjoying her day. This morning it seemed like she wasn't having a good time. She walked in with bags underneath her eyes and she was in a mellow mood. She's been a bit odd all week, come to think of it. I'm worried about her. Gabby has finally disappeared from our lives and I thought she'd be happy about it, but she's been acting strange instead.

Emilia glances up at me before blowing out the candles, and for a second I wonder if she thought of me when she made her wish. She and I only have a couple of months left together before I'll leave for college, and I hope she wants to spend them with me the way I want to spend them with her.

Emilia cuts the cake and frowns a little. She looks up at her dad with disappointment, but hides it instantly and smiles. She hands everyone a slice of cake and then takes a bite of her own slice. She struggles to mask her disgust, and her smile looks awkward, but it seems like only Kate and I notice. Kate discreetly swaps her empty plate for Emilia's and I sigh in relief.

"Told you she'd love the cake," her dad says, pointing at her empty plate. I blink in disbelief and nod slowly. How can the man be this clueless?

I wait patiently for the evening to end. It's not obvious to anyone but me and maybe Kate, but Emilia is definitely not having a good time. She was delighted at the start but her excitement waned quickly — her mood is back to what it was this morning. Her smile doesn't reach her eyes and she looks impatient for the day to end, but I'll be sure to change that tonight.

Chapter Twenty-Eight

EMILIA

I'm tired. Exhausted, really. Ever since Kate made me promise to never fall for Carter, my heart has just felt broken. I can't sleep, I can't eat. All I can think about is him, and how badly I want to be with him. I'm not even excited about my own birthday, and until a week ago I'd been counting down the days diligently.

I get into bed eagerly. I can't wait for this day to be over already. Kate and Helen have tried their best to give me a good day, and the spa day we had was really fun, but I just couldn't enjoy myself. It's like no matter how hard I try, my heart isn't in it.

I've only been in bed for a few minutes when I hear my bedroom door open. I sit up in surprise. My dad seemed dead tired when we got in, so I didn't think he'd come to my room. My eyes widen when I see Carter standing in my doorway.

"Are you crazy?" I hiss. He and I are both dead if my dad catches us. Carter shrugs and holds up one of his hoodies. He pulls me out of bed and pushes the hoodie over my head.

"Your birthday isn't over yet, baby," he whispers. Carter pulls me along and out of the door quietly, pausing long enough for me to get my flip-flops on. He leads me straight to his car and grins as he buckles me in.

"What are you doing? Where are we going?"

Carter smiles. "It's a surprise," he tells me. I'm instantly excited. I love surprises, but I guess I'm also excited to spend some alone time with him. He and I haven't spent a single second alone since I made Kate that promise. But tonight, I'm weak. Tonight, I need a high enough dose of Carter to sustain me for the foreseeable future.

Carter is quiet as he drives us towards the nearby woods, but his excitement is palpable. I can't help but be ridiculously excited too. When we finally reach our destination, he takes out a flashlight before running around to get me. Rather than helping me out of the car, he lifts me into his arms. He pushes the car door closed with his hip and carries me into the woods, one arm underneath my knees and one arm supporting my back.

"Hey, are you murdering me and burying me out here?" I whisper.

Carter chuckles and winks at me. "Only one way to find out."

I giggle and hide my face against his neck. Carter laughs and I hug him tighter. I can see some sort of light in the distance and I peer at it, trying to figure out what it is. I gasp when he carries me into the clearing.

He's set up a large blanket surrounded by pillows, with a large hanging sheet in front of it that seems to act as a big screen. He's somehow created a small little private theatre for us, lit up by dozens of lanterns. It looks ridiculously romantic and my heart melts. I can't believe he did this for me.

"This is amazing," I whisper, hugging him even tighter. Carter smiles at me indulgently and puts me down on the blankets before joining me. He grabs one of the folded blankets and throws it over my bare legs. When he abducted me I was wearing sleeping shorts and a tank top. His huge hoodie is comfy and warm, but my legs and feet were a little cold.

Carter seems nervous and flustered as he fidgets with a bag that he had hidden away here.

"Just how long did it take you to prepare all this?" I ask, truly awed. Carter shrugs.

"Not that long," he says, clearly lying. Eventually he reveals what he's been hiding, and I gasp.

"You got me a chocolate cake!"

He puts it down in front of me and sticks a candle in before lighting it. He clears his throat awkwardly and then starts singing, his voice low and soft.

"Happy birthday to you, happy birthday, my dear Emilia... happy birthday to you," he sings, his cheeks bright red. My heart beats a thousand miles an hour and I wish I could capture this moment. Then I realize I can, and I fish my phone out of his hoodie to take a photo.

"Smile," I whisper, making him pose with my birthday cake. He looks like he wants to decline, but in the end he indulges me and does as I ask. He shakes his head while I stare at the photos I took happily.

"Make a wish, Minx," he says.

I nod and lean in, making the same wish I made earlier today. I wish for Carter, Kate and I to all be happy. I blow out the candle and Carter hands me a spoon.

"I forgot to grab plates, but I've got a spoon," he says. He smiles awkwardly and I take it from him. I hold out a bite for him and his lips close around the spoon. He takes it from me and then holds it out in front of me to offer me a bite. Just as I'm about to lean in, he smears cake all over my lips.

I gasp.

"You... you devil!" I shout. Carter bursts out laughing.

"I'm sorry, baby. I just couldn't help myself," he says. Carter leans in and pinches my chin gently. My heart starts racing when he smiles at me before kissing the edge of my lips. I feel his tongue glide over my skin and I inhale sharply. He sucks on the edge of my lips and groans softly.

He makes quick work of the smeared cake, and I'm all worked up by the time he's done with me. So close, yet he didn't actually kiss me. I sigh when he pulls away. He's breathing hard, so at least I know he's as affected as I am. He reaches back into what I've dubbed his bag of mysteries and takes out a small cardboard box. I frown when he puts his phone inside it, only to look up in amazement when I realize that the flimsy little box acts as a projector; a pretty good one, at that. The hanging sheet instantly transforms into a movie theatre screen and I look at it excitedly as Carter puts Netflix on.

"So, I have it on pretty good authority that The Notebook is the cheesiest chick flick out there, A.K.A Google told me. Do you wanna watch that, or should we watch something else?"

I hesitate for a second. I actually don't even like The Notebook all that much, but I'll watch anything with Carter. "Yeah, let's watch that."

He puts it on and then rushes back to me. I lift the blankets, and he joins me underneath them while he props some pillows up behind us. I lie down in his arms and look up at the screen, but all I can think about is how close he is to me. He's wearing sweats and a tee, and all my mind can focus on is how easy it'd be to get those off. We haven't gotten together in months now. We've both done our best to stay friends and nothing more, but I know he wants me as much as I want him.

Carter squirms when I shift in his arms. Every time I get closer, he pulls away a little. It's frustrating as hell. Eventually I get the hint and push away from him. I try my best not to pout or sulk. I don't want him to feel pressured into giving me something he doesn't want to. I wrap my arms around myself and hug my knees to my chest, turning myself into a little ball. He's salvaged the train wreck that was my birthday, and I still have the gall to feel upset. Maybe my dad was right. I really am ungrateful.

"Hey, what's wrong?" Carter asks. I look up at him and shake my head, trying my best to smile at him as innocently as I can. I don't want him to know how rejected I feel. He frowns and pulls me back to him. He lies on his side so we're both facing each other.

"Tired?" he asks. "I know it's late... we don't have to do this. We can just go back if you want. I didn't really think about how tired you might be. I literally pulled you out of bed."

My body is so close to his and my heart is racing. He looks at me with his gorgeous hazel eyes and I fall a little deeper. I'm done for. My hand cups his cheek gently and he blinks, startled, but he doesn't move away from me.

Would it be okay if I'm just selfish tonight? Would it be okay if I just forget about Kate and our families for a single night? I bite down on my lip in contemplation and Carter's eyes follow my every movement. His breathing accelerates and he swallows hard. I'm as acutely aware of him as he is of me. My eyes drop to his lips, and I move in a little closer. Just one kiss. Would that be too much to ask for?

"Emilia," he whispers. I look into his eyes and find the same desire reflected in them. I lean in closer until my lips brush against his. That's all it takes for Carter to snap. He captures my lips with his and rolls on top of me, pinning me down with his weight. I moan in delight when he pushes his hard on between my legs.

"Fuck, Emilia," he whispers. His tongue slides over my lips, and I open up for him, tangling my tongue with his. I'll never get enough of the way he kisses me. His hands roam over my body until they find their way underneath his hoodie and I moan. He holds me right below my chest. I whimper a little and he chuckles as his fingers glide over the underside of my breasts. I didn't think he could get any harder, but he does. The way he's pushing against me is almost painful.

"I want you," I whisper. "Just for one night, Carter. Can I call you mine just for tonight?"

He pauses and pushes himself up a little to look at me, the sweetest smile on his face. "Emilia, I've always been yours. I'll always be yours," he says solemnly. If only that could be true. I sigh and pull him back to me, his lips crashing against mine. It reminds me of the way I awkwardly kissed him that very first time, and I giggle against his lips. Carter smiles and kisses me while my hands roam over his body. I pull his t-shirt up and he stops kissing me only long enough to let me take it off.

I don't stop there, and he soon realizes what I'm up to. He looks at me heatedly as he helps me take off the hoodie I'm wearing, and the rest of our clothes soon follow. At last we're naked together for the first time since we went skinny dipping, and it couldn't have felt more perfect. Carter settles back on top of me and his erection presses against me. He rests his forehead against mine and inhales deeply.

"I want to touch you," he whispers, and I nod eagerly. Carter smiles as his trembling hand traces my inner thigh until he's finally touching me where I want him. He kisses me and moans when he realizes just how wet I am.

"Fuck, Minx," he whispers. I feel frantic and turned on beyond reason. I need him to touch me. I need more. I look up at him pleadingly and he grins when his fingers find their way between my legs. They brush against my slick heat and a soft moan escapes my lips. "You're really wet, Minx," he whispers. I feel myself blush as he pushes a finger inside me. "Emilia, I don't really know what I'm doing," he admits nervously. He seems anxious and clumsy, and I can't help but giggle against his lips. I place my hand over his and guide his fingers so his thumb touches me right where I want it. He keeps up the movements I showed him, and I slowly but surely lose control.

I'm frantic as I boldly wrap my hands around his erection. I still remember how he touched himself, how he pumped up and down until he lost control. In my mind I've replayed the scene I watched over and over again, imagining that it's my hands touching him in his bed. Now I finally get to do it.

The pace Carter touches me with increases and within minutes I'm close.

"Carter, I can't hold on," I whisper. He deepens our kiss and smothers all my moans with his lips. I moan his name as I shatter and Carter's eyes fall closed. Seconds later he comes all over my stomach. The way he's panting afterwards and the little whimpers that escape his lips are hot as hell. He drops his forehead to mine and smiles at me.

"Fucking amazing," he whispers, and I nod shyly, in full agreement. I giggle and he laughs before kissing me again. He sits up and reaches for his bag.

"I brought napkins... they were actually for the cake," he says awkwardly. He wipes me clean and then lies down, opening his arms for me. I settle into his embrace as he yawns.

I look up at him and smile. I can't remember the last time I was this intensely happy. I lift my face and kiss his cheek gently. I'm filled to the brim with love and affection. I'm not sure I can even hold the words in much longer. It's like those three little words are fighting to burst out. I want to tell Carter that I love him, but I know it wouldn't be fair to say it when I know we can't be together. I know Carter wouldn't be able to live with himself if he and I ended up making both Helen and Kate unhappy. The love and respect he has for his mother and sister is one of the things I admire most about him. Neither one of us would be able to forgive ourselves if our dating destroyed the delicate balance that's in place now.

Carter and I stay cuddled up together and actually manage to watch the remainder of The Notebook. I don't think my birthday could've been any more perfect. If only things could always be like this between us.

Chapter Twenty-Nine

EMILIA

I walk into the living room and smile when I see Carter lying on the couch. He's wearing sweats and a tee, his hair a mess. He looks hot. He glances up when I walk in and smiles at me.

"Hey," he says. I'm secretly thrilled to find him alone. I was hoping I would. Ever since my birthday, we haven't been alone for a single moment. Every time I think we'll have just a few seconds together, Kate interrupts us. It's almost like she's developed some sort of sixth sense that alerts her whenever Carter and I get too close. Or maybe it's a sign. Maybe the universe is trying to tell me I'm doing the wrong thing here. I know I am, but it's so hard to stay away from him.

"Come here," he says, rising from his seat, his voice husky. I grin and run up to him, crashing into his arms. Carter laughs and wraps his arms around me, hugging me tightly. I rise to my tiptoes and he looks into my eyes. The way his eyes twinkle tells me he feels the same way I do. I just know it. "I can't even remember the last time I got to hug you," he whispers. "I miss you."

I melt against him and tighten my grip. "I miss you too," I

whisper, truly feeling it as well. Even though I'm right here in his arms, it still feels like it isn't enough.

Without overthinking it, I press my lips against his. Carter kisses me back instantly and I smile against his lips. I've wanted this for so long. He threads his hand through my hair and I sigh happily.

A door opens near us, and we jump apart. Helen walks in seconds later and pauses, her eyes jumping between us suspiciously. She looks at us through narrowed eyes, but thankfully ignores our awkward behavior. She hasn't brought us dating up again, but almost getting caught reminds me it's not just Kate I'm betraying. It's Helen too.

"You're here early, Milly. Kate is still asleep," she tells me. I nod as though I didn't already know that. She looks at Carter with raised brows. "And you're up awfully early. Usually I can't get you out of bed until noon."

He looks away embarrassed and glances at me with a sweet smile on his face. Surely he isn't up early because he too was hoping we might have a moment together? Carter shrugs and his mom shakes her head knowingly.

"Hungry?" she asks him. He looks at her in disbelief and she laughs. "Of course you are." She tips her head towards the kitchen and we follow her in.

"You look beautiful," he whispers. His eyes trace over the spaghetti straps on my dress, his eyes darkening instantly. It's obvious what he's thinking. If his mom wasn't right here, he'd be pushing those straps out of the way. I glance down to find him hardening. He looks at his mom anxiously and then readjusts himself to hide his arousal. I burst out laughing and he glares at me, but I can't help it.

"What are you doing today?" he asks, his eyes roaming over my body. I'm too embarrassed to admit that I dressed up for him.

"Nothing much. Kate and I said we'd hang out. Feels like we haven't hung out in a while. I think she said she wanted to go shopping or something? I'm not too sure. I just want to spend some time with her. I miss our friendship and the way we used to be. She's always been like a sister to me, but recently it's almost like we've become strangers. I know hanging out won't fix that, but I think it'll be a step in the right direction."

Carter sighs and shakes his head. "Minx, I don't know. You'll both need to put effort in, but her more so than you. You're not the one that ditched her over Gabby, so don't take on all the responsibility of saving your friendship. Kate needs to work at it too."

Helen smiles at me and nods. "Carter is right. It breaks my heart to see what you two are like these days. You used to do everything together and now it's like you barely know each other, but that isn't your fault Milly. I saw how hard you tried and how Kate pushed you away. I've always said that I love you as my own daughter, and I mean that. Don't ever feel obligated to remain friends with anyone that doesn't treat you right - Kate included. My door will always be open to you, Emilia. I would love for you and Kate to go back to how you used to be, but I don't want you to feel forced to do anything."

My heart feels so full it might burst. I've known Helen for years, yet she never ceases to amaze me, she never fails to make me feel loved and welcome. I feel terrible for what I did on my birthday and then again this morning, after she asked us not to get together. I can't believe I betrayed her the way I did when she's only ever been amazing to me. I'm terrified of losing the only real mother I've ever really known, and this time I'll be to blame. My heart hasn't recovered from my own Mom leaving, and I don't think I'll survive losing Helen too. Especially if it's because of my own actions.

Carter nods and hands me a glass of orange juice. Helen looks at us with wide eyes and I pause before taking a sip.

"You..." she says. "You didn't put anything in Emilia's glass, did you?"

I blink and look up at Carter suspiciously, but he shakes his head. Come to think of it, he hasn't pulled a single prank on me lately, and I haven't pulled any on him. Usually we'd never dare accept any food or drinks from each other. I take a cautious sip, but it doesn't seem like there's anything wrong with it.

Carter laughs and shakes his head. "I swear, Minx. I didn't do anything," he says. I look at him through narrowed eyes and hand him the glass.

"You drink half," I order. Carter shrugs and empties half the glass in one go before handing it back to me.

I sip my orange juice in silence while Carter devours his breakfast, offering me a bite or two every once in a while. Eventually Kate comes storming into the kitchen. She looks surprised to find me here already, and I wonder if I'm being slightly suspicious.

"You're here," she says, glancing at the clock. It's only eleven, and on weekends I usually don't come over until one. I nod and move away from Carter to sit next to her instead. I see him frown from my peripheral vision but thankfully he doesn't say anything.

"I was thinking of hanging at the shopping center today. I wanted to buy a new dress for my birthday. Maybe we can go to Starbucks too?"

I nod, already imagining the caramel frap I'll have later. I can't wait. I'm not a huge fan of shopping, but Kate's obsessed with it.

"I'll drive you. I need to drop by the shopping center to grab some sports gear anyway," Carter says. Kate freezes and looks at him with furrowed brows before nodding slowly. She then looks at me, and my heart hammers in my chest. I have a feeling she might be onto us, and it terrifies me. Carter and I aren't dating. We aren't really anything, but our lips are definitely too intimately acquainted. Other parts of our bodies, too. I know we've already taken things too far, and I feel incredibly conflicted about it. I'm racked with guilt, but I also can't stay away from him. It's like he's the air I need to breathe, and even though I try to resist, I feel like I'm not truly alive unless I'm with him.

I'm nervous as we make our way to Carter's car and linger behind purposely so that Kate ends up in the backseat. I open the passenger door and she frowns at me.

"What are you doing?" she asks. I look at her in confusion and she throws me an annoyed stare. "Carter said the whole rule about one of us sitting in the front is out the window, right? Why would you sit in the front?"

I glance at Carter, and he looks as exasperated as I feel. He grits his teeth and is about to turn around to look at her, but I shake my head subtly to tell him to keep quiet. I sit down next to Kate and she smiles at me. Something is off, though. Her smile is somewhat calculative, and I'm worried she might know something.

Carter parks the car and Kate jumps out almost immediately. She pulls me along and waves at Carter. "Thanks, bro," she shouts. "We'll text you later to see if you're near so we can hitch a ride home."

Carter looks startled, and it's obvious he was planning on spending some time with us, or with me, maybe. He nods at her and sighs before walking off in the opposite direction.

"That's nice of him, to drop us off," she says as she hooks her arm through mine. I nod, scared to reply too strongly. She seems on edge somehow.

"Don't you think?" she adds. I nod again.

"Yeah, I guess."

Kate laughs humorlessly. "I guess you're used to it. When you're around, he always drops us off. When I was with Gabby, he'd straight up refuse."

Her words grate on me and I can't help but want to stand up for Carter. "That has more to do with Gabby than it does with me. I'm not all over him like she always was."

Kate looks at me with raised brows and an unamused smile. "Aren't you?" she says. I bite down on my lip and shake my head. I'm unable to deny it vocally — I'm unable to lie straight to her face. Just a week ago I was touching Carter in places I shouldn't have been. Just a week ago I was lying underneath him, and just this morning his lips were locked with mine.

"Yeah, you wouldn't. You promised, after all. Our friendship would be over if you ever broke your word. I'm sorry, I know you're not Gabby. I'm just thinking too much."

I gulp and nod at her, trying my best to smile. I know Kate well enough to know this is a thinly veiled threat. I'd never risk my friendship with her or my relationship with Helen, which means I'll have to work harder at letting go of Carter before it's too late.

Chapter Thirty

EMILIA

"Ugh, I totally failed calculus again," I mutter. Kate loops her arm through mine and shakes her head.

"Let's just wait for the results because you say this every time and you usually do really well."

I shake my head and pout. "Not when it's calculus."

No matter how hard I try, I'm barely scraping by. Kate drags me to the picnic benches behind school and I follow listlessly. She stops all of a sudden and stares at one of the tables with such fascination that I can't help but follow her gaze. I'm surprised when I find Asher at the receiving end of her interest. He and Carter are sitting at a table scattered with papers. I can tell from the way Carter grits his teeth he's frustrated, so they're probably working on their college essays. He's incredible with scientific subjects, but he absolutely hates anything for which there is no one correct answer. Creative writing and essays are his nemesis and he'll usually have his mom and me read over his essays multiple times before he'll submit them. He looks ridiculously cute and my heart skips a beat as I try to drag my eyes away from him. I glance back at Kate, but thankfully she's still too focused on Asher to have noticed my little slip.

"You like him," I say. Her head whips towards me and she looks at me with wide eyes. "You like Asher, don't you?"

Kate shakes her head. She looks conflicted and guilty as she looks away, unable to hold my gaze.

"You know I won't tell Carter, right?" I say, my voice soft and kind. She looks up at me pleadingly and I can see internal torment flashing through her eyes. For a second she looks devastated.

"I know, Milly. I'm sorry. I wasn't trying to keep it from you or anything... I just didn't know how to bring it up."

I know all too well how she feels. I've been wishing I could talk to Kate about Carter because it just doesn't feel right to keep it from her, and on top of that, I miss talking to her. There are so many things I would've loved to giggle and joke about with her, but I can't — because it's Carter.

"I tried not to, Milly, I swear. I've been staying away from him as best as I can and nothing is going on at all. I could never do that to Carter, you know. But I also can't help how I feel. I'll get over it at some point. Once Asher leaves for college, I'll get over it for sure."

I hesitate before I speak and turn towards her nervously. "I don't think Carter would mind it that much, you know. He trusts and likes Asher, I doubt he can think of a better guy for you."

She looks at me in confusion and shakes her head. "No way, Milly. He'd never be okay with it. That's like you dating Carter. I'd never forgive either of you, so I just know my brother would be the same. He'd never forgive me. Besides, what if we dated and then broke up? I don't want to be the reason things get awkward between Carter and Asher. Not that it could even work out with him going away and all."

The reminder that Carter is going to college soon hurts. When he leaves, he'll forget about me. I know he thinks he won't, but I know what it's like. I can barely even remember my mother, and I know she definitely forgot about me. If my own mother can forget about me, then Carter and I don't stand a chance, especially because we aren't even dating.

I nod and Kate tugs on my hand. "But we can hang out with them, right?" she whispers.

I laugh. "Of course, Kate. You don't ever need an excuse to hang out with your own brother, you know."

She looks up again as though she only just realized that Carter is there too, and I bite back my smile. Kate has been on dates before and she's had crushes before, but this is the first time I'm seeing her act so flustered and cute. She tugs on my hand and leads me to the table, her palm clammy against mine. I can't believe that she's so nervous just walking towards Asher.

Carter looks up when we approach and his eyes roam over my body. I blush under his gaze and he smiles at me, making the butterflies in my stomach go wild. A single look from him has my heart beating in overdrive... it's ridiculous.

"Hey," he says. He takes his bag off the bench to create space for us and scoots closer to Asher. Kate's smile drops a little, and I wonder if I should create an opportunity for her to sit next to Asher instead. Before I can do so, Carter pulls on my hand to get me to sit next to him. The edges of my lips tug up as I take a seat while Kate sits down next to me. Both of us take out our textbooks to study with the guys.

"How was your test?" Carter asks.

I groan and shake my head. "Don't ask."

Kate looks at us, her eyes moving from Carter to me, before settling back on her textbook. She purses her lips and looks away.

"How did you do, Kate?" Asher asks her. She looks up in surprise and smiles at him, and it isn't until then I realize Carter asked *me* how the test went, but not her. She nods at Asher and smiles as she answers him.

Carter pushes his essay towards me and underlines a couple of phrases. "What do you think, Minx?"

He leans against me so that my shoulder is against his chest and I long to lean back against him, to be wrapped in his arms. I can barely focus as I read through his essay. My attention is shot entirely when Carter bursts out laughing and holds his phone up for me.

"Look at this," he says. I stare at the Baby Yoda meme and shake my head. Carter loves everything Star Wars related and he'll laugh at every single Baby Yoda meme he comes across.

"That's not even funny," I say, even though I'm smiling. It *isn't* funny, but I can't help but smile when he laughs like that.

Kate tries to look at his phone, but he doesn't notice and pulls it back before she manages to take a look. Kate's expression clouds over and she closes her book with force before shoving it into her bag and walking off. I jump up and run after her.

"Hey, what's wrong?"

She pauses and turns around to face me, her expression a combination of anger and sadness. "Why are you even following me? It's not like you need me. Seems like Carter and you have plenty of fun and inside jokes together. It's like I'm not even your best friend anymore. You two keep shutting me out and making me feel like I'm an outsider."

I blink in disbelief and hold her by her shoulders. "Kate, what are you talking about? That's not true at all. Of course you're still my best friend."

She looks away. "Milly," she says. "I've told you I'm sorry, so why do you still punish me for what happened with Gabby?"

I let go of her, shocked. "What are you talking about?" I ask. "I didn't do anything, Kate. It's just that Carter and I became closer friends while you were friends with Gabby. You'd go out with her and you didn't often invite me along so Carter would hang out with me instead. That's all it is. I don't really know what I've done wrong or how I can even fix it. What am I supposed to do, Kate?"

She shakes her head and lowers her eyes, but not before I catch a glimpse of the tears gathering. I always knew that I'd be hurting Kate if Carter and I got together. If she's this hurt from me being close friends with him, which is all we're trying to be, then she'd truly never get over it if he and I dated. It hurts to know that I'm causing her pain, yet I can't help but still want Carter despite it.

"You haven't done anything wrong, Milly. I'm just — I'm just jealous, I guess. That's part of why I started hanging out with Gabby in the first place. I love you, Milly, but sometimes it feels like my family loves you more than they love me. You're so close to Carter that it's like you're now his best friend instead of mine, and my mom always asks for you before she'll ask for me. I know I'm being crazy but still..."

I nod and wrap my arm around her shoulder. "I'm sorry, Kate. I didn't realize you felt that way. If you want, I can stop coming over so often? I don't know."

I sigh in relief when she shakes her head. "No, Milly. You're part of our family. You always have been. It's my fault that there's so much distance between us and between me and my family. It's because I let Gabby get between us, and I'll work on fixing it myself. I just thought you should know how I'm feeling and why I sometimes get angry when you haven't done anything. I know it's not fair and I'll work on it. Don't you worry about it."

I smile at her and nod. So long as Kate puts in even the slightest amount of effort, everything will fall back into place. I have full faith that it will.

Chapter Thirty-One

CARTER

Emilia comes rushing into my room and closes the door behind her. I sit up at my desk, startled. Her cheeks are flushed and she's panting, as though she ran all the way here. She looks stunning, and I've missed her like crazy. The last few months have been tough.

I've had to put my all into school and football, and on top of that Kate has been keeping a good eye on the two of us. Forget pranks or kisses, I've barely been able to have a single full conversation with my Minx.

"I heard you got scouted," she says, her chest rising and falling. I look away and nod. Word travels fast, I see. I was going to tell her myself, but it looks like someone beat me to it.

"Sort of, but not exactly. Coach got in touch with the Coach at USC to come and watch me play. God, Minx. I've never been more nervous, but it was so worth it. They offered me a partial athletic scholarship. Can you believe that? They said the award letter would likely arrive today or tomorrow. If everything goes to plan and my grades don't slip, I'll get a partial academic scholarship too, and between them, most if not all of my college fees will be covered. I'm so relieved, Minx. You have no idea. Football scholarships are usually renewed every year, though. If I get injured or don't perform well enough, I might be at risk of not graduating, but I'm trying not to worry about that for now."

Emilia nods and walks up to me. I wrap my arms around her waist. Just holding her sets my heart at ease.

"Carter, I'm so proud of you," she says. "You have no idea. I've seen firsthand how hard you've worked for this, and I'm so happy it all worked out."

I blush and pull her closer to hide my embarrassment.

"You're honestly so impressive," she continues. "I don't know anyone that's got football offers *and* might also get an academic scholarship. Carter, you're the best."

I grin and bury my head in her chest, and she laughs. "It's only *one* football offer, Minx. It'd be much more impressive if I could get a full scholarship for either, but I'm very happy with this."

"Where are you touching?" she whispers. I press a kiss to her chest and she giggles. A shrill sound interrupts us, followed by the sound of someone rushing up the stairs. Emilia and I pull away from each other seconds before my mother storms into my room, her face flushed.

"It came," she says, her eyes wide. My heart drops. Mom doesn't even have to tell me what it is. I know exactly what she's talking about. The letter offer letter from USC is here. I follow her down the stairs. I didn't think I'd be so nervous, but I am.

My parents, Kate and Emilia are all seated around the dining table as I stare at the letter from USC. It's my dad's alma mater, and the school both Kate and I have always wanted to get into, but if I didn't get the academic scholarship, I won't be able to attend. What if I open it and it says I've been awarded the athletic scholarship, but not the academic one? Emilia smiles at me and nods.

"Open it," she whispers. I pick it up with trembling hands.

My dad hands me the letter opener and I slice through the envelope. It takes me ages to read it. I stare at it in disbelief. I don't know how much time has gone by, but everyone's expression falls one by one. My parents and Kate look at each other, worried, but Emilia grins and takes the letter from my hands.

"Congratulations," she reads out. My dad exhales in relief and claps me on the back.

"Had me worried there, kiddo," he says. My mother squeals and Kate looks at me like I just hung the moon and the stars. Emilia smiles at me as though she never had any doubt I'd make it. She hands me back the letter and I put it away carefully. My family hugs me one by one, and finally Emilia is in my arms. She hugs me tightly and presses her lips against my throat.

"I'm so proud of you," she whispers. I tighten my grip on her and smile widely. I hold her much longer than I held anyone else and don't pull away until my dad clears his throat. Emilia blushes and I smile. Staying away from her in the last few months has been tough as fuck. It doesn't help that she keeps looking at me like she's thinking about the things she wants to do to me. I'll take every second that I can get with my Minx.

Mom grabs a bottle of champagne while dad hands each of us a glass. "This is a special occasion and definitely a reason to celebrate so you can all have a few sips," Mom says, filling up our glasses. I've waited for this day for what seems like forever. We all toast and celebrate. Everyone is just as happy as I am. If anything, my parents might actually be even happier. Even mom's strict no drinking rule is out the window.

Emilia slips onto the patio with her champagne glass in hand, and I follow her. The warm breeze blows through her hair and ruffles her satin skirt. She looks stunning, and she looks hurt. I walk up to her and wrap my arms around her from behind. She stiffens and turns in my arms, startled. She was so lost in thought she didn't even notice me.

"Carter," she says, her voice tinged with longing. I smile down at her and wrap my hands around her waist. She places her palms on my chest and steps closer to me. "Congratulations," she murmurs.

I grin and dip my head. "Hmm... shouldn't you reward me for my accomplishment?" I whisper. My eyes fall to her lips and Emilia looks at me with blazing eyes. The need between us is palpable.

"We shouldn't," she says. My lips brush against hers and she gasps softly.

"Make an exception for me, baby. It's been so long."

Emilia rises to her tiptoes and kisses me. Her arms wrap around my neck and she pushes her breasts against me. I groan and tangle my hand in her hair, pulling her as close as I can get her. I kiss her deeply, our tongues tangling together. The way she moves her body against mine drives me crazy. She giggles when my hard on presses against her stomach.

Emilia's lips are on mine when the door opens behind us. We spring apart before my mom walks out. We're both acting awkwardly, but thankfully mom ignores our behavior. I'm sure she knows something is going on or she wouldn't have asked us if we were dating, but I'm grateful she isn't on us the way Kate is. Mom hands me her phone with a wide smile.

"Grandma wants to speak to you," she says. I smile and take the phone from her while Emilia blushes and disappears back inside. My heart is still hammering when I walk back into the house. Emilia is sitting next to Kate and looks up when I walk in.

"I'm proud of you, son," my dad says. "I knew you'd get in. You've worked really hard and it's paid off, kiddo."

My mom nods and throws her arm around my shoulder. "My little boy is all grown up now," she says. I shake my head and blush — so embarrassing. Kate and Emilia giggle and I glare at them. I'm glad to see Emilia smiling. Lately, her mood seems to drop whenever anyone mentions me going away to college. It takes a couple of days to drive home from USC so it won't be easy for me to come back often, and it'll be two years before Emilia and Kate join me, if they end up getting into USC at all. Things will change soon. We won't be able to play pranks on each other, and I won't have any more stolen moments with her. I won't see her every day anymore. A lot can change in the two years that we'll be mostly separated. I'm not sure what things are going to be like between us. Would we text and call? Would we stay in touch at all? I can't imagine my life without Emilia, but I have no idea what our future holds.

Chapter Thirty-Two

EMILIA

I stare at the stack of neon pink post-it notes and smile. Kate looks at me and shakes her head. "He's going to kill you," she says. She drops to the floor and extends her legs as she stuffs a handful of popcorn into her mouth. I can't believe she actually brought popcorn.

I grin and start pasting post-it notes to Carter's car. It'll take me forever to do, but it'll be so worth it.

"It's gonna be so weird when Carter and Asher are gone. I'll really miss them," she says, a sad expression on her face. I nod and smile sadly.

"Me too."

Kate hasn't told me anything, but I've seen the way she and Asher have been like at school. The two of them have been acting a bit suspicious, and lately she's grinning at her phone more and more often. I'm not a hundred percent sure what's going on, but I have a feeling they might've acted on their feelings somehow. I wouldn't be too surprised if they kissed or something. I'm a bit hurt that she's keeping something from me, but I have no right to be mad at her since I'm keeping so much more from her.

I have a feeling Carter suspects something too, but just isn't calling them out. Part of me feels conflicted about her thinking that it's okay to go behind Carter's back like that, but being unwilling to even entertain the idea of me with him. I've been wanting to talk to her about it, but our friendship barely survived Gabby and I don't really want to put it to the test again so soon.

"I don't know, Milly. I mean, they're going to college. They're both football players and they'll be living in a frat house. I'm sure they'll go out a lot, and there'll be girls. I know Asher and I aren't together, but I just don't like the idea of girls trying to seduce him. What if Carter asks him to wingman and stuff like that?"

My heart drops. She's right, of course. Carter will probably start going out a lot — he might even start dating. The idea of Carter drunk and messing around with some girl tears me apart. In the last couple of months, he and I have threaded a fine line. We've kissed a few times, but mostly we've managed to stick to being just friends. Neither one of us has so much as flirted with someone else since the Gemma incident. We aren't dating, and we aren't even together at all, but it seems like we have an implicit agreement of sorts.

Kate drops her head to her knees and sighs. "I have no right to even. I know Asher and I will never be together, but I also can't stand the idea of him being with someone else. I'm so selfish, Milly."

I shake my head and look down at the floor. "You're not self-ish, Kate. You're in love. It's okay not to be okay, you know? I know you have feelings for Asher, and letting him go will hurt. But like you said, you two can't be together, especially since he's leaving soon. There's no point in agonizing over it. Just enjoy the time you have left with him as best as you can."

She looks up at me fearfully. "I think I really am, you know. In love, that is."

She drops her head back to her knees to hide her flushed face and I bite back a smile. She's being so cute that I kind of want to tease her about Asher.

"I know," I say instead. "I noticed the way you've been smiling at your phone, and I've seen the dozens of notifications on your phone — all from Asher. I kind of figured you were going down that path."

Kate pouts and looks away, ignoring my comment altogether. I know what she's like. She won't want to face her feelings, especially because he's leaving soon. My arms are starting to get sore from the post-it notes and I stretch them out for a minute. I've covered half of Carter's car already, transforming it into a bright pink. It looks ridiculous and I love it.

"Will you miss Carter?" Kate asks. I'm startled by her question and blush. It almost feels like a trap.

"Yeah, of course I will. We've seen each other almost every single day since I moved here, and I've always loved pulling pranks on him. It's going to be pretty weird once he's gone. We might argue a lot, but I actually see Carter as one of my best friends. He's annoying as hell, but he's always there for both of us. It'll just be weird."

Kate nods and sighs dramatically. "I don't like how everything is changing," she says. I'm glad she isn't questioning me further. I wonder if she's letting it be because she's now in the same position I'm in. I nod at her and continue to paste post-it notes to the car. As I stick the last one on, Carter walks out of the house with his car keys in hand. I jump up, surprised, and Carter stares at his car, open-mouthed.

"Surprise," I yell.

I start running, but Carter catches up to me quickly and throws me over his shoulder. I squirm in his hold and giggle. He grabs my ass and holds me in place. I look up to see Kate running into the house. I can't believe she abandoned me and left me to deal with Carter's fury.

"I needed to run to the store, but if I have to drive around in that monstrosity then you have to as well. You're coming with me, Minx."

He opens the passenger door and drops me into the seat before running around the car. I groan, embarrassed, and buckle myself in.

"I can't believe you did this," he says, laughing as he pulls out onto the road. "How many damn post-it notes did you use? How long did this take you?"

I giggle. "Hundreds. It took over two hours, but the look on your face was so worth it." I glance out the window, frowning. "Hey, I thought you said we were going to the store?"

Carter shakes his head and glances at me. "We're not," he says, his voice low. I stare at him with wide eyes. "Now, what should I do with you? I can't believe you violated my precious baby this way."

I laugh and roll my eyes as he parks the car in the middle of nowhere. He grins at me and unbuckles my seat belt. My heart is racing and I'm certain he's going to kiss me, but instead he pulls back. He crosses his arms over his chest and glares at me. "So, how should I punish you for making my car *pink*?"

I feel myself blush and shrug, but my heart is beating wildly and I'm filled with anticipation. The way he looks at me tells me he wants me as much as I want him.

"I'm sure you can come up with something," I whisper, my eyes dropping to his crotch. He's acting all cool, but he's really hard.

Carter grins and leans into me, his lips brushing against mine. A soft moan escapes my lips when he finally kisses me. He deepens the kiss and pulls me closer. His tongue tangles with mine and his hands roam over my body. He pushes his seat back and looks at me, beckoning me over with his fingers.

"Come here."

I smile and climb over, settling in his lap. He's so deliciously hard. He groans when I rotate my hips against his and he buries his hands in my hair, pulling slightly. The kiss slowly turns into more and Carter's hands settle on my ass.

"You know we can't," I whisper. He bites down on my lower lip and all my protests are long forgotten. I have such strong convictions — when he isn't right there to make me forget all about them. When he's within reach, I can't resist. I keep wanting one more touch.

"I can't stay away, Emilia. I need you," he says. He drops his forehead against mine and closes his eyes.

"Do you know how hard these last few months were for me? I'm leaving soon, baby. I've only got a couple of weeks left with you. I can't stay away, I won't do it. Not when I know you want me just as bad."

His lips find mine again and my hands slip into his t-shirt. Carter pushes his hips up to thrust against me and I moan against his lips. His hands fumble with the button on my jeans. Just as he's got it open, his phone rings. We both jump, startled. He grabs his phone and groans when he sees that it's his mom.

It's like a bucket of cold water has been thrown over me. I scramble back into my own seat while he answers the phone. It sounds like she's giving him a list of things to buy and I bite down on my lip. We're gonna have to go to the store now, and we'll need to be home soon. He looks up at me when he hangs up.

"I'm serious, Emilia. I'm done staying away from you. If you feel the same way, then meet me at the treehouse tonight at ten."

Chapter Thirty-Three

EMILIA

I stare at my watch. It's ten past ten, and I don't know what to do. I want to meet Carter at the treehouse, but I'm also scared. I glance out the window. The treehouse looks dark, so he might not even be there. But what if he is? What if he's waiting for me?

I stare out the window for a couple of minutes and finally make up my mind. I'm as quiet as I can when I walk past my dad's bedroom. I sneak out of the house and walk up to the treehouse, my steps almost soundless. I pause at the stairs and look around me. My heart beats harder with every step I take.

I gasp when I finally walk into the treehouse. Carter covered up the windows and filled the inside with fairy lights. He's put pillows and blankets on the floor, making the entire space look cozy. He's sitting in the middle of the makeshift bed and looks up at me.

"I thought you wouldn't come," he whispers. I shake my head and kick off my flip-flops before stepping onto the blankets. Carter seems nervous and cups the back of his neck.

"I wasn't sure," I murmur. He smiles and extends his legs while I drop to the blankets beside him.

"So why did you come?" he asks.

I blush and look away. "Because I'm done staying away from you too."

I know it isn't the right thing to do and my heart feels conflicted about letting down Kate and Helen, but I think I might love Carter more than anything or anyone else in the world. No matter how hard I tried, I couldn't stay away. Not tonight.

Carter grins and pulls me closer. "Thank god," he says, right before he kisses me. He leans into me and I fall back onto the floor, my head on one of the pillows. He moves on top of me and spreads my legs with his knee. I bury my hands in his hair and pull him towards me, my lips crashing against his. He moans when I throw my leg around his to get him closer.

Carter's hand moves to my breast and he kneads softly. I arch my back, wanting more, and he gladly obliges. He grabs the hem of my dress and pushes it up. I raise my hips to help him take it off and his eyes widen when he takes in my matching red lace underwear. His eyes roam over my body hungrily and I can't help but blush.

"You too," I whisper, tugging on his t-shirt. Carter nods and pulls his t-shirt off with ease. It's like he gets hotter every time. The extra hours of football practice have made him even more muscular. My hands slide down his abs until I reach his jeans.

I undo the button, and he looks at me with wide eyes. "You want that off too?" he asks. I nod at him and Carter blushes more. He takes his jeans off and settles back on top of me in his boxers.

He kisses my neck and I moan when he kisses me in a spot I never knew was sensitive. He chuckles and moves down to my collarbone, taking his time exploring my body. "Fuck, Minx. You have no idea how many times I've imagined doing this to you. Kissing your body like this."

He reaches around me to undo my bra and fumbles with it, unable to get it open. He curses and I start to laugh. I push my chest up and reach behind me to undo it myself. He looks embarrassed. I take the bra off and Carter inhales sharply.

"You're so beautiful, Emilia," he whispers. He lowers his lips to my breast and takes my nipple into his mouth. The way he swirls his tongue around it sends bursts of pleasure through my entire body.

"Carter," I whisper. He smiles against my skin and moves further down, kissing my stomach and then the top of my panties. He pushes my legs up and kisses the inside of my thigh. I'm trembling, blinded by desire. I need him to touch me already. I don't think I've ever been this turned on before.

He kisses me between my legs, right through my panties, and I moan loudly. He chuckles and does it again. I'm panting and he looks up at me as he grabs the edges of my panties. I nod and he slides them off slowly. He moves back up and settles on top of me, his lips on mine. I'm nervous and self-conscious now that I'm lying underneath him naked. My hands roam over his body until I'm holding the waistband of his boxer shorts. Carter pulls away a little to look at me.

"We don't have to go any further, Minx. I have no expectations or anything, I just want to spend time with you. I'll happily kiss you all night and do nothing more than that."

My heart melts and I tug on his boxer shorts more urgently. He chuckles and eventually shrugs out of it nervously. I gasp when he's naked and move to grab his erection, staring at it fearfully.

"You'd never fit inside me," I murmur. Carter laughs, the awkwardness fading.

He leans on his side, lying half on top of me, and lowers his head to mine. He kisses me so gently that my heart feels ready to burst. His fingers trail over my skin until they slide over my wet folds. I gasp when his thumb finds my clit — he now knows exactly how I like it. I can barely think straight when he's touching me like that. Within minutes, he's got me ready to burst.

My muscles spasm around his fingers and he smothers my moans with a kiss.

"Carter," I whisper. He looks into my eyes and tilts his head in question. I'm almost too embarrassed to say it. "I want you. I want to do it."

His eyes widen, and he gulps. "I... I... Uh, are you sure?"

I bite down on my lip. "Don't you want me, too?" I ask.

Carter takes my hand and wraps it around himself. "What do you think, baby?"

I giggle and pull him closer. He reaches for his jeans and pulls a condom out of his pocket. I look at him through narrowed eyes and he rushes to explain. "I bought some today. I thought maybe... I don't know."

His ears are bright red, and his hands tremble slightly. I giggle and sit up as he rips open the packaging. He tries to roll the condom on, but it won't roll down easily. He looks up at me with bright red cheeks and looks beyond flustered. I laugh and rise to my knees, my hands closing around his.

"Let me try."

He nods, and after a few tries I manage to roll it down.

"So tight," he murmurs. He grimaces, and I'm worried we might've done something wrong.

"Is it okay? We don't have to..."

Carter looks at me and grins mischievously. "Baby, are you crazy? I'm pretty sure I've waited for this all my life."

Chapter Thirty-Four

CARTER

"Carter, I want it," Emilia whispers. I grin and push into her slightly. She's soaking wet and feels amazing. I'm scared I won't be able to last more than a few seconds. I don't want our first time to be over so quickly, but I don't know if I'll be able to control it.

Emilia gasps, her eyes widening. She's tight around me, really freaking tight. I push into her a bit deeper and slide inside with relative ease. I pull back and then push into her all the way in one go. Emilia whimpers in pain and I freeze. Tears gather in her eyes and I panic.

"Baby, are you okay?" I whisper. She nods, but her face is scrunched up in agony. I don't know what to do to make it better.

"Fine. I'm fine," she lies. I lower my face to hers and kiss away her tears.

"We can stop, Minx. We don't have to do this. If it hurts, let's just stop."

Emilia shakes her head and tangles her hands in my hair, grabbing tightly. She pulls my face to hers and kisses me, shutting me up. I hold myself up on top of her and kiss her slowly and sweetly.

She relaxes underneath me after a couple of minutes and I pull back a little to thrust back into her. Her face scrunches up in discomfort, but at least it looks like she isn't in pain anymore.

"Shit, Minx. I'm so sorry. I don't know what to do."

Emilia throws her arms around me and shakes her head. "I'm okay. I want this, Carter. Please don't stop now."

I nod and thrust in and out of her slowly. I've been ready to come since the second I pushed into her. She feels amazing around me, so fucking tight and so ridiculously wet.

"I can't, baby. I won't be able to last long. I'm sorry," I groan, dropping my forehead to hers. She giggles and kisses me. My restraint dissolves and I moan as I thrust into her harder and quicker.

Emilia looks into my eyes as I come harder than I ever have before. I moan her name and collapse on top of her, completely spent. She hugs me and I bury my face in her hair. "You always smell amazing," I whisper.

Emilia laughs. "It's the perfume you buy me every year. I love it."

I inhale deeply and pull out of her. She looks surprised to find me softening, and I'm embarrassed. I turn around and grab a tissue from my pocket. The condom is coated with a small amount of blood, and I take it off carefully before joining Emilia on the blankets.

"That was probably much better for me than it was for you," I say grumpily. She laughs and rolls on top of me while I reach for a blanket to cover us with.

"It was good," she says, and I can't tell if she's lying. I feel both horrible and delighted at the same time. It was amazing for me, but I'm so embarrassed that I couldn't make it good for her too.

I caress her body as we snuggle together. "I did sort of have hopes that we might do it," I admit. "But I actually just wanted to talk to you and hang out with you."

She rolls onto her side to look at me and throws her leg over

165

mine. "I'm going to miss you, Emilia. I'm going to miss the way you mess with me, and I'm going to miss seeing you every day. I'm going to miss your smile and the random conversations we have."

She looks sad and pulls me closer, hiding her face in my neck. "I'm going to miss you too, Carter. I'm so used to seeing you every day. Life won't be the same without you. Will you call me when you're away?"

I nod and lower my head to kiss her. Her lips linger on mine and I sigh. "Of course I'll call you, Minx. We can video call and shit."

She smiles and presses another kiss to my lips. I pull away a little to look into her eyes and inhale deeply. "I want to be with you, Emilia. I want you to be mine, officially."

She looks at me with wide eyes and blinks. "Carter, you're leaving soon," she whispers. I drop my forehead to hers and sigh.

"I know, I know I am. But can't we just try?"

She looks at me excitedly, but then her expression drops and I know she's going to reject me.

"I want to, but it's probably not a good idea," she says. "Kate would never forgive me. She made me promise, you know. After the whole Gabby thing, she made me promise to never fall for you. I can't break her trust like that, Carter. Especially not now that our friendship is finally recovering. Besides, your mom told us clearly that she didn't want us dating either. We'd be breaking both their hearts, when we won't even be able to be together. You're going to be so far away that we won't ever see each other. Besides... you'll be at college. It'll be different. You won't want to be tied down by a girl in your little hometown."

I'm worried about Kate and Mom too, but I truly believe they'll get over it, eventually. She hasn't said it, but I know Emilia is also worried that I'll suddenly start drinking and sleeping around. As if I have time for that with my school workload and football.

"Emilia, you know I'd never cheat on you. In the last couple of months we weren't even dating, yet I didn't even look at any other girl. You're the only one for me, Minx."

She bites down on her lip and I see the insecurity in her eyes. "Carter, being in a long-distance relationship would be really hard. I'm worried we'd hurt your family if we dated and then broke up. I'm not sure my friendship with Kate would survive, and I'd be letting your mom down too. Your mom has never asked anything of me, you know? It's bad enough that we're going behind her back like this, but it's something else entirely to start dating knowing we don't have her blessing."

I sigh and pull back, holding myself up on top of her. "Do you really think we can go back from this? That we'll be able to act like we're just friends now that we've slept with each other? I *know* you want me too, Emilia. I know you want to be with me. So, why won't you? Kate will get over it, and I know Mom loves you enough to accept our choices. But, you know, we don't even have to tell them if you're worried about their reaction."

She gulps and looks away. She seems torn, and I know I shouldn't, but I blame my family for this. The main reason she won't be with me is because of Mom and Kate. It doesn't help that Emilia seems convinced I'll forget about her once I go to college. Like that would ever happen. I wonder if she thinks that because of her mother. How do I make her see I'm not anything like that woman?

"We can, Carter. We can still be friends now. There are no hard feelings between us. I just... I don't think we should date."

My heart fucking shatters. I close my eyes and push away from her. I grab my clothes and get dressed in record time. I feel like I might actually cry. There's nothing I want more in life than to be with Emilia. If she felt an ounce of what I feel for her, that'd be enough for me.

"Carter!"

I glance back at her and shake my head. "We would've been so good together, Emilia. If only you'd give us a chance."

I walk away and run a hand through my hair, frustrated as hell. She broke my fucking heart, but I still want to go running back to her.

Chapter Thirty-Five

CARTER

Emilia walks in and pauses when she sees me sitting in the living room. I hate how stunning she looks. I hate how that dress she's wearing hugs her body. I hate that all I want to do is walk up to her and kiss her silly. I want her in my arms with her hair tickling my neck. I hate how badly I want her — I still remember the way she felt wrapped around my dick, the way she moaned my name and the look in her eyes when she told me she wanted me. I can't believe she slept with me and then told me she doesn't want to date me. I offered her my heart on a silver platter, and she trampled all over it. I understand why she did it, but that doesn't make it hurt any less.

"Hey," she murmurs. She stands by the doorway instead of walking in, as though she wants to keep as much distance between us as possible. I look away and glance back at the TV.

"Uh, have you seen Kate?"

I don't look up at her, even though my entire body is begging me to. I still have a small amount of pride left, and I cling to it with all my might.

"Nope."

I see her fidget awkwardly from the corner of my eye, and I'm almost ready to give in. She seems fine with breaking my heart, yet I can't even stand to see her feeling remotely uncomfortable.

"But it's Wednesday. We haven't missed marathon day in a while. Not since... not since Gabby."

I falter and turn to look at her. Why does she have to be so beautiful? Her blonde hair shines golden in the sunlight coming in from the window, making her look like some sort of Goddess. Her eyes are darker than usual and she looks seductive as fuck. Emilia doesn't usually wear much makeup, but today she looks a little dolled up. I can't help but hope that it's for me.

"Well, she's not here," I reply, looking away.

Emilia freezes, and it takes all my willpower to stay seated. I want to walk up to her and wrap her in my arms. I want to hug her and hold her close. I want to feel her lips against mine. Above all, I need just a small sign that she wants the same, yet she gives me nothing.

"Hey, you're here," Kate says. She almost walks into Emilia and drags her into the living room with her. "Oh, you're wearing makeup."

Emilia blushes and nods. "I did one of those YouTube tutorials you sent me. It was actually pretty hard."

Kate squeals excitedly. "It looks so good though! I knew you'd get the hang of it quickly."

Emilia nods and I roll my eyes. So it wasn't for me then. She didn't get dolled up for me. Why the hell do I keep getting my hopes up? I'm such a fucking loser.

Kate reaches for the remote control and I grab it to keep it out of her reach. "What the hell, Carter?" she shouts. She jumps up to grab it from me, but I hold on to it.

"What's wrong with you? You know we always do marathon days on Wednesday."

I shrug. "I don't care. I'm watching TV. Go watch at Emilia's house or something."

The last thing I want is for Emilia to leave, but I know it's probably better that she does. Part of me is hoping she'll fight me, though. I want her to tell me I'm being a dick, to see that fire in her eyes as she demands that I hand over the remote. I glance over at her, but she's sitting on the sofa demurely as though Kate and my antics have nothing to do with her. My mood plummets even further.

"How can you be so mean to me, Carter? I'm literally only asking for the TV on Wednesdays. You have it pretty much to yourself most other days. Just one day, damn it. Can't you even give your sister that much?"

I roll my eyes. She's always watching Netflix, not just on Wednesdays. I'm sick and tired of Kate's shit. "I told you I don't care. Go watch somewhere else. I'm watching the game."

Kate crosses her arms and glares at me before throwing puppy eyes my way. Her expression goes back to rage when I don't give in.

"Come on," she says. "I'm not feeling that well. I think I might have a cold coming up. I just wanna lie down and chill for a bit."

I glance at Emilia, who is finally smiling. Her eyes catch mine and she nods.

"Yeah, she's totally got an upcoming cold," she says, not at all convincingly. I stare Kate down and she purses her lips.

"I don't see why you'd get priority access to the remote control just because you're feeling ill, though. Just go to bed."

Kate looks at me in disbelief and then looks at Emilia. "Milly, help me out here," she pleads. Emilia hesitates and then rises to step closer to me. Her perfume washes over me and my heart instantly starts to race.

"Carter, please," she says. "We always do marathon days on Wednesdays, and you know that."

"I don't care." I shrug, looking her straight in the eye. Emilia looks startled, probably because I've always given in whenever she's asked me something. Even Kate looks surprised.

She glances at Kate and smiles tightly. "Let's just go to my house." She turns to leave and I grab her hand to stop her. She looks back at me and I hand her the remote. I don't want her to go. Even when I'm mad at her and I want to get a rise out of her, I still want her near.

"I can't believe you two are being such cry babies about it," I snap. Emilia's lips turn up at the edges and she takes the remote from me. She looks up at me gratefully and it hits me right in the chest.

I'll never be able to deny this girl anything. If our roles were reversed and she was the one asking me out, I'd never be able to say no. I'd do everything in my power to keep our relationship secret if that's what it takes, but I'd never deny her. The fact that *she can* tells me enough about where I stand.

I need to get over Emilia. I need to nip my growing feelings in the bud. I need distance and I need space. I can't be around her, at least not for a little while. I need to forget about her.

Chapter Thirty-Six

EMILIA

"Are you sure he'll let us stay?" I ask, oddly nervous. Kate puts on another coat of lipstick and drags my already far too revealing dress down a little more, showcasing even more of my boobs.

"Carter is holding his graduation party at our house and *begged* Mom and Dad to go away for the weekend. Since Mom isn't here, he's stupid if he thinks he can keep us away," she says.

I shake my head as she sticks her hand into my bra to adjust my boobs for maximum cleavage. I look in the mirror and smile to myself. She's actually done a great job. We both look good. Kate looks stunning with her long brown hair and miniskirt. She's managed to make me look so much hotter too, with the makeup and the push-up bra. I feel like a totally new person — I can't even remember the last time I felt this confident. I wonder what Carter will think when he sees me. Things between us have been a little weird. He's been ignoring me, and I've been trying my best to pretend that my heart isn't breaking. There have been no pranks, no texts, no conversations, and definitely no kisses or longing looks. It's like he got over me the moment he realized I didn't want to be in a relationship with him. It hurts, but I can't even fault him for it.

The party is already in full swing by the time we walk down the stairs. Kate's eyes light up when she sees Asher, and he looks just as excited to see her. These two are going to get caught soon if they don't hide their obvious attraction better. I'm worried about them and at the same time I want what they have. Kate told me about their first kiss a few weeks ago and how guilty she felt about it, but just like Carter and I, she and Asher can't seem to stay away from each other. She tells me it's just a fling and that they'll break things off as soon as Asher leaves for college, but I know it's more than that for her. I'm worried Carter will find out about them and kill them both. For a while I was sure he knew about them, but now I'm not so sure. Part of me also hates that Kate is doing the one thing she said she'd never tolerate. Why is it okay for her to get with Asher, even just for a few weeks, but I can't do the same with Carter without risking my friendship with her and my relationship with Helen? It's unfair and I hate it.

Kate looks up at me pleadingly and I sigh, trying my best to put my bitterness aside. Even if I can't have what I want, I shouldn't begrudge Kate her happiness. I smile at her and nod, earning me a grateful grin in return. It only takes her a couple of minutes to disappear and she's being far from subtle. I'm worried she and Carter will both get hurt over this. Mostly Carter... I'm scared he'll feel betrayed when he finds out about Asher. Part of me is also concerned that he'll blame me for knowing and not telling him.

I inhale deeply and walk into the kitchen to pour myself a vodka with cranberry juice. I've only taken three sips when Carter comes storming into the kitchen. He looks hot as hell. He's wearing a shirt that's tight enough to showcase his muscles, and he's got the sleeves rolled up to show off his forearms. I want to unbutton his shirt and reveal what he's hiding underneath. Weeks have gone by since we slept together, and even though he's been acting like I don't exist, I still crave him with the same desperation.

Carter looks at me, his eyes glued to my chest. I guess my cleavage at least got him to look twice. He blinks a few times and then drags his eyes back up to mine.

"Oh, no you don't," he says, grabbing the cup from me. I glare at him and he glares back at me just as fiercely. "What the hell are you doing here, Minx? And what the actual fuck are you wearing? *A t-shirt?* Where are the rest of your goddamn clothes?"

I look down at my dress and then back at him. "It's a dress, *dad.*"

I grab my drink back and take another sip. Carter looks at me through narrowed eyes and takes it from me.

"You'd better go now before I throw you out."

I grin and fish my phone out from between my breasts. Carter looks at my chest with wide eyes, his cheeks suspiciously pink.

"Oh, hmm... it's quite noisy here. I think I could hear the music from my bedroom. I wonder what Officer Oliver will think if I call it in?"

He grabs my wrist and glares at me. "Don't you fucking dare, Minx," he snaps. I smile at him triumphantly and take another sip of my drink. "No more," he says. "This is the only drink you get. You can stay, but you'd better not cause any trouble."

I nod happily, and he sighs as he walks back out. My eyes linger on his disappearing form. His ass looks great in those jeans. Ever since we slept together, Carter and I have been further apart than ever when we should've gotten closer instead. He seems hurt, and he's been avoiding me more and more recently. It kills me, but I know I had it coming. I knew what would happen when I told him I didn't want to date him, so I need to suck it up and deal with the consequences.

The girls from the cheering squad are all here, and they instantly surround Carter. Thank God Gabby isn't here, at least. Though I have no doubt she'll be showing up later. He's always kept an appropriate amount of distance from her, but will he still?

If she throws herself at him tonight, will he just go for it the way he did with Jennifer?

If the mere thought of that makes me jealous, then how the hell would I be able to have a relationship with him when he's all the way at USC? I'd just be wondering where he is and if he's even thinking of me. I don't want to do that. The risk is too high. It's not just me that would get hurt if things didn't end up working out. It's Helen and Kate too.

I finish my drink and join a couple of rounds of beer pong, which I'm surprisingly bad at. Jace, one of Carter's teammates, laughs at me and wraps his arm around my shoulder.

"This game isn't for you, sweetheart. Looks like you're already well on your way to being drunk, and we're only a couple of hours into the party."

He leads me towards another group of people and sits me down.

"Spin the bottle?" I ask, feeling myself blush. Carter is the only guy I've ever kissed. My mind flashes back to Jennifer. He might be my only kiss, but I'm certainly not his.

"Sort of. It's kind of a combination of spin the bottle and seven minutes in heaven. Whoever the bottle lands on is the person you get locked up with in the bathroom for a couple of minutes. You don't have to do anything and you can decline if you want to, but might be good fun."

I hesitate, but then I sit down. What the hell, it's just a game. Carter seems quite happy to be chatting with the girls that keep surrounding him. Other than when I first walked in, he hasn't spoken a word to me. Why shouldn't I have some fun too?

As I sit down, my eyes meet Carter's from across the room. His eyes flash when he realizes what game we're playing, and he stalks towards me. He sits down right next to me and throws his arm around my neck. He pulls me closer until his lips brush over my ear and a delicious little shiver runs down my spine.

"What the fuck are you doing playing this game, Emilia? I thought I told you to stay out of trouble."

Someone spins the bottle and it points towards me. The guy looks at me excitedly, but Carter shakes his head.

"You'd better fucking spin again, buddy," he says, a far too relaxed smile on his face. The guy nods, much to my annoyance. I don't even know him and would've just made small talk if I ended up in the bathroom with him, but that isn't the point.

I grab the bottle and spin it, my teeth clenched. My heart skips a beat when it points to Carter. He chuckles and pulls me up by my wrist. I follow him into the bathroom nervously. He keeps the lights off and locks the door before turning towards me. Carter cages me in with his arms, and even with my heels on I'm nowhere near as tall as him.

"So, what exactly did you think would happen if you played this game, Minx?"

He takes a step closer until his body is pushed against mine. I put my hands on his chest, unsure whether I want to push him away or pull him closer.

"Were you really going to kiss some other guy? Someone I know? At my own damn party?"

He leans in until his lips are hovering over mine. "Answer me, Minx."

I shake my head. I was being petty because Carter has barely looked at me all night. Because he's been ignoring me for weeks. Because it seems like he's already over me when my heart is still filled with him.

I look into his eyes and his lips brush against mine.

"No. Just you, Carter," I whisper.

His lips come crashing down on mine roughly, and I rise onto my tiptoes in a silent bid for more. When his tongue presses against my lips, I open up for him eagerly. Carter's hands find their way to my ass and he lifts me into his arms. He presses me against the wall and I wrap my legs around his hips.

"This dress is way too fucking short, Minx."

His fingers slip into my underwear, and I moan against his lips.

I fumble with his jeans and sigh in delight when I finally have my hand wrapped around him. Carter groans and kisses me harder.

"I want you, Emilia," he whispers. I'm panting and nod. He grins and rests his forehead against mine.

The sound of someone knocking on the door startles us both and we freeze.

"Time's up, guys," someone shouts. Carter blinks and looks around, as though he's only now realizing that we're in the downstairs bathroom. He pulls away from me and lowers me to the floor carefully before fixing his own clothes.

"Sorry, baby. I got carried away," he says, panting. I shake my head and rise to my tiptoes to press a quick kiss to his lips.

"I wish it'd gone further," I whisper, right before I walk out.

Chapter Thirty-Seven

CARTER

I watch Emilia as she walks around the room, socializing and drinking. Every once in a while she touches her lips and smiles to herself. That little smile of hers makes my damn heart skip a beat. One kiss, and my resolve crumbled. I've done my best to stay away from her, but a single touch puts me back at square one. I'm crazy about her.

Emilia keeps glancing around the room, obviously in search of my sister. If I'm not mistaken, Kate is still locked up in her room with Asher. The two of them have been wrapped up in each other for weeks now, both of them convinced that I don't know about them. Though the idea of those two together makes me uncomfortable, I can't really be mad about it either. Not when I'm head over heels for Emilia. I'm more concerned about Kate hurting Asher than I am about him breaking her heart. I'd rather not think about what exactly those two are getting up to, but I doubt they're dating. It'll be two years before Kate will join us at college if she gets in at all. She'll need to work her ass off if USC is her aim.

Emilia sways on her far too high heels and makes her way towards the stairs. I'm worried she'll break her damn neck. I glance around the room. There aren't that many people left. I walk up to one of the juniors on my team and clap him on the back.

"Make sure everyone leaves in the next hour or so. The door locks automatically, so don't worry about that. Make sure no one breaks anything, all right?"

He looks at me in awe and then nods, his eyes lighting up with his new duty. I just about keep from rolling my eyes and follow my Minx up the stairs. She's nowhere to be seen. I pause at Kate's door and try the door handle, but her door is locked.

"Kate? Are you in there? Is Emilia with you?"

Silence. My annoyance rises instantly. I *know* Kate is in there. She hasn't left her damn room all night.

"I have a spare key, Kate. Don't make me fucking use it. Is she with you?"

I hear something crash in her room and then she finally answers me. "No! She's not here. Don't come in right now, I'm changing!"

Changing, my ass. I check all the rooms on the floor before walking into my own bedroom. I sigh in relief when I find her curled into a ball on top of my bed. I walk up to her and take her heels off gently. She stirs and looks at me. She looks hot as fuck, all sleepy and relaxed.

"Want me to take you home, baby?"

She shakes her head and sits up. My dick springs to attention when she tugs on her dress and eventually pulls it over her head. Her body is phenomenal. I'll never get enough of seeing her like this. I lick my lips and force myself to look away. I grab one of my t-shirts from my closet and walk back to her, only to find that she's ditched her bra. She's sitting on my bed, looking so fucking seductive.

Emilia takes the t-shirt from me but doesn't put it on. Instead, she rises to her knees and starts tugging on my clothes.

Her hands run over my chest and she bites down on her lip. She looks into my eyes and my heart feels so full it might actually burst. Emilia grins and undoes my buttons one by one, exposing my chest and then my abs. She's hyper focused on her task and I lose myself in her beauty. Her shoulder-length hair is pin straight and the makeup she's wearing today makes her look so seductive. She's always beautiful, but tonight she's breathtaking.

Once she's got the buttons open, she pushes my shirt over my shoulders and leaves it hanging there, her attention captured by my abs. She sucks on her lower lip as her palms slide over my skin, her fingers trailing down my abs. I tense underneath her touch. I can barely think straight when she's touching me like this.

"Take it off," she whispers. She looks up at me pleadingly, her eyes hazy with lust. I oblige and ditch my jeans before tugging off my shirt. Emilia smiles and pulls me towards her. I join her in bed and she pushes me flat on my back before straddling me. She looks so fucking stunning with her hair falling to her shoulders and her tits on full display. I reach up to cup them and play with her nipples, making her moan. She lowers herself on top of me and kisses me. She tastes like tequila.

"Baby, I think you're quite drunk. We shouldn't do this, not when you're drunk," I whisper.

Emilia laughs softly and kisses me again. "Shut up, Carter," she says. "I've waited too long for this. All those weeks of you ignoring me... I've had enough."

I groan and roll us over so I'm on top of her. She tugs on my boxer shorts and I take them off, making quick work of her panties too. My dick rubs up right against her slick heat, both of us finally naked. She threads her hand through my hair and pulls my lips onto hers. I kiss her and she rolls her hips up underneath me.

"We need a condom, baby," I whisper against her lips.

She groans in dismay when I pull away to grab one from my nightstand. I put it underneath my pillow for later, but Emilia shakes her head.

"Put it on now," she whispers. I frown and do as she asks.

"Let me play with you first, Minx," I plead.

She shakes her head and moans softly. Her body is trembling with need.

"I want it now, Carter. Please." I grit my teeth and align myself to push into her. She moans in delight when I sink into her, her eyes filled with passion. She wraps her legs around me and I sink into her even deeper. I'm relieved to see that she's clearly enjoying it this time. She's fucking soaking wet. I thrust in and out of her slowly, angling my dick in such a way that she gasps every time I move back in. She looks so fucking hot right now.

Emilia pulls me closer and kisses me.

"So good," she whispers. Her hands roam all over my body. She grabs my ass and pulls me back into her harder and I fuck her rougher. She moans into my ear and I almost come right then and there. She pulls me closer and puts her lips against my neck, sucking and biting as I increase the pace.

"Yes, Carter," she whispers. The way she moans into my ear drives me insane.

"I'm gonna come, baby," I whisper. She nods and moves her lips back to mine, smothering my moans. I collapse on top of her and she grins happily, stroking my back as I try to calm my raging heart down.

I take care of the condom before lying down next to her. I smile down at her and move my hand between her legs. Emilia moans when my thumb rubs over her clit, and within minutes I've got her coming hard too. She looks so hot lying in my bed like this.

She smiles up at me seductively and I peck her lips. I take her into my arms and hug her tightly. Emilia shivers and I grab the t-shirt she threw on the floor and hand it to her.

"Wear this, baby. You'll get cold," I whisper. She nods and pulls it on while I grab my boxers from the floor.

I open my arms, for her and she settles against me. Everything feels so perfect with her in my arms like this.

"Carter," she whispers.

"What's wrong, Minx?"

"I don't want you to leave," she whispers, squirming in my hold. "Can't you just stay?"

Her pleading tone goes straight to my heart and I instantly want to promise her I will, but I know I can't. Would things have been different if she'd asked me a few months ago? Maybe I could've put more effort into making her mine.

"It's just two years, Minx. In two years you'll be right there with me, giving me hell. I'm sure you'll make college completely unbearable for me. I'm already looking forward to it."

"I'm going to miss you, Carter. Some days I feel like I'm closer to you than I am to Kate. My life won't be the same without you."

I bury my hand in her hair and gently kiss her forehead. "I'll come back often, Minx. I promise. You can visit me whenever you want, too."

She shakes her head and hides her face in my neck. "It won't be the same," she whispers. Emilia sighs, her lips brushing against my neck. I hold her until her breathing evens, and then I finally close my eyes.

Chapter Thirty-Eight

EMILIA

I'm startled awake by a loud bang, and Carter tightens his arms around me. He clutches his bed covers and throws them over us. My head is banging and the whole world is spinning. I'm still drunk or hungover like crazy. What am I even doing in Carter's bed? In his arms?

I stiffen when I realize we're all tangled together. His arms are around me, while my arm is wrapped around his waist and my leg is hooked over his hip.

"*Carter Christopher Clarke.* You'd better not have a girl in that bed or so help me God! You know the rules," Helen shouts. I stiffen in Carter's arms. It's one thing to fall asleep in his bed, and it's something else altogether to get caught like this. I've never heard her sound so angry.

"She said *Christopher*," I whisper. "We're in so much trouble."

Carter chuckles and buries his hand in my hair to pull me closer.

"Mom, I'm tired as hell. There's no girl here. Of course there isn't. If I was gonna do something like that, don't you think I would've already done it by now?"

I can't help but hope that his words are true and that he truly hasn't had anyone other than me in his bed. With the distance he created between us in the last couple of weeks, I wasn't sure. It seemed like he was moving on, and part of me is terrified he might have done something with someone else. Even if he did, I can't be mad about it. It's me who said that we shouldn't be together, after all.

"Then explain to me why the hell there are heels and a dress on your floor?" Helen bites out. I freeze and look down at my clothes. I'm wearing one of Carter's t-shirts. *Shit*. I try my best to remember where I threw my clothes, but I'm drawing a blank. I can only remember flashes, almost like scenes popping into my head randomly. Carter and I kissing in the downstairs bathroom. Me walking into his bedroom. My fingers unbuttoning his shirt. The way he sank into me and the way I begged him to do me harder. I blush in shame, the night coming back to me slowly but surely.

Carter strokes my arm and pulls the sheets down to reveal his face while still keeping me covered. "Mom, please. Fine, I've got a girl here. I'm sorry. It's not what you think though. I didn't sleep with her or anything. I mean... We literally just fell asleep. That's all."

I can imagine the way Helen must be staring him down. She always knows when Carter is lying, though I still haven't figured out *how*. "Oh, you just fell asleep and did nothing else, but you got her naked first?"

Carter groans and hugs me tightly. "Mom, can you please just go? This is so embarrassing. It won't happen again, *fuck*. I'm literally moving out today. What does it matter?"

My heart sinks at the reminder, and I subconsciously clutch his t-shirt in my hands. Helen clears her throat.

"Of course it matters. Until this day is over, you still live under my roof, so you better damn well follow my rules. If she had the guts to sleep in my house without my permission, then she'd better have the guts to face me the morning after."

I poke his chest and he lifts the sheets just slightly to look at me. I try my best to look at him reassuringly, but he shakes his head and covers me up again.

"Mom, please," he says, throwing all his charm at her, but she won't relent, like I knew she wouldn't. I sigh and push against him before sitting up. The sheets fall away and I blink a few times to get used to the light.

Helen looks beyond shocked to see me in Carter's bed. "I'm sorry," I stammer, my face burning. "I didn't mean to intrude, Helen. I told my dad I'd sleep over at Kate's, but she was already asleep when I walked in and you know how she sleeps, all sprawled out... I was so tired last night and I fell asleep here. My dress was uncomfortable so Carter gave me one of his tees," I explain, pointing towards the t-shirt I'm wearing. I feel horrible for lying and I'm sure my rambling isn't helping my case, but I don't know what else to say. Helen blinks at me, her eyes moving from me to Carter. "I should've just gone home, I know. I'm so sorry."

She stares us both down and my heart races. I'm not sure we'll get away with this. She seems mad as hell, and I'm not sure she'll actually believe our excuses. Her eyes roam over our clothes on the floor and she chuckles humorlessly, as though she knows we're lying. "So, nothing happened, huh?" she asks me. I shake my head at the same time as Carter. "Hmm," she says, thoughtfully.

She crosses her arms and stares at us through narrowed eyes. "I'm going to let it go this time, and I'm choosing to trust you. You two better not betray that trust."

Carter and I both nod. Helen is intimidating as hell, and there's no way I'll voluntarily find myself in another situation like this.

"So, what do you wanna have for breakfast?" she asks, relaxing slightly. "Seems like you two got drunk, huh? I'd better get some carbs into you. Come down in a couple of minutes." We both nod, and she walks out of the room, closing the door behind her.

I fall back onto the pillow and Carter looks at me. We both stare at each other and then burst out laughing.

"Shit. I thought your mom was going to throw me out," I say, exhaling in relief.

Carter laughs. "Nah, she adores the hell out of you. Any other girl, though... Yeah. She probably would've thrown out anyone other than you."

He turns onto his side and looks down at me.

"Is it true?" I ask. "What you said?"

Carter frowns, clearly not following.

"That you haven't had a girl in this bed? You were being so distant with me... I wasn't really sure. I mean, if you did, I can't even be mad at you. So, yeah."

Carter looks away and smiles to himself. "No one but you, Minx. I can't even imagine wanting someone else, even when you drive me insane. Besides, my mom's always home during the day anyway, so it's not like I could ever get away with it. I've never had a girl in this bed. Other than you, that is. Forget the bed, there's only you, Emilia. I haven't touched anyone else."

I smile up at him and poke his chest. "You'd better not have," I say. Carter laughs and hugs me tightly, neither one of us wanting to get up. He lowers his lips to mine and I promise myself that this will be the last time I'll kiss him, but my heart knows that I'm lying to myself.

Chapter Thirty-Nine

CARTER

Emilia and Kate both look so fucking sad as Asher and I pack up the car. I'd love to think that my sister is sad I'm leaving home, but it's not me she's concerned about. Nope, she's looking at my best friend with heartache in her eyes. Part of me wishes they'd stayed away from each other a little longer. If they waited until they were both at college, they might've actually stood more of a chance. Asher looks as torn up as she does. They're being so obvious that it's hard for me to pretend like I don't realize they've been getting together behind my back for weeks now. He wasn't even being subtle when he suggested we pick his stuff up first and then mine. It's obvious that doing it that way around means he gets to say goodbye to Kate, which he wouldn't be able to do if I went to pick him up after I was done here.

Emilia, on the other hand... Her sadness is all for me. Part of me is still nervous, though. If I know my Minx at all, she'll have one more trick up her sleeve. My mother bursts into tears as I put the last box in my trunk. I sigh and wrap my arms around her. It's always been my mom that's wrapped her arms around me. When did our roles reverse? When did she start to feel so small in my arms?

I hug her tightly and try my best to keep my heart from breaking. I hate seeing my mother cry. I don't usually care about women crying, but there are three women in my life I can't stand to see in tears. My mother, Kate, and Emilia.

"Maybe I should come with you — I could drive you there. What if there's something wrong with your accommodation? We don't know, right? We should check. What if you need something?"

I look at Emilia pleadingly and she takes on the role my sister is too heartbroken to assume. She puts her arm around my mother's shoulder and hugs her tightly. My mother turns towards her and throws herself into Emilia's arms. Emilia almost stumbles back from the impact, but smiles nonetheless.

"Milly," my mom cries. "Tell him to stay, Milly. Just one more day," she pleads. Emilia looks at me and I know that if she asks me to, I'll do it. For a second I think she will, but then she shakes her head.

"He can't stay, Helen. Asher and Carter have already stayed for as long as they could. Their orientation is soon. They have to go today," she says. She rubs my mom's back and part of me wishes my dad was here today instead of at work. I'm sure it's going to be tough for my mom. Emilia looks at me reassuringly and I know my mother is in good hands, but it still hurts to leave them behind.

"Mom, you'll be fine. I can either drive or fly back whenever you want me to, and you can come visit me whenever you want. Don't cry like that," I tell her. She nods and throws herself back into my arms. I laugh and hug her tightly.

"My baby. You're all grown up now," she says. I smile at her. She's embarrassing the hell out of me, but she's my mom, and I love her.

"Yes, Mom," I murmur, patting her back. Eventually she steps aside and I open my arms again to hug Emilia. She hesitates for a second before she launches herself into my arms. She looks at me, her arms around my neck. My eyes automatically drop to her lips, my mind replaying the way I kissed her at my leaving party, the way those soft lips of hers tasted and the way she moaned my name hours later. I drag my eyes away. I pull her closer and drop my face to her neck, pressing a sly little kiss to her skin. She sighs and tightens her hold on me.

"I'll miss you, little Minx. I'm sure college will be boring without you. Hurry up and join me, okay?"

She nods and rises to her tiptoes. For a second I'm sure she'll kiss me, but then she presses her lips to my cheek. I smile when her lips linger. Will things always be like this between us? I know she said she didn't want to date me, and I have no choice but to accept that. But might she change her mind someday? She and I are so good together... I know I'm too young to know for sure, but I'm pretty sure my Minx is *it* for me. Maybe I'll be able to convince her through phone calls once I'm away. Maybe she'll miss me and she'll realize just how silly she's being. I'm reluctant to let go of her, but eventually she steps back and my sister takes her place.

"I'll miss you, douchebag. You and Asher take care of yourselves and each other, okay?"

I smile to myself. It's obvious to me she's only concerned about Asher, but I won't call her out on it. I'm sure it's hard enough on that Asher is leaving today.

Emilia has her arm around my mother as Asher and I drive away. Today should be one of the most exciting days of my life, so why does it feel like I'm leaving my damn heart behind?

I accelerate and hear something crack underneath my foot. Seconds later, the entire car fills with a horrible smell. Asher coughs and opens the window. "Smokeless stink bomb? Fucking Emilia!" he shouts. I chuckle.

"Good one, Minx," I say to myself as I pull over to air out the car. I'm going to miss her like fucking crazy, and I may need to look into ways to pull pranks on her from a distance. There's no way I can go without my dose of Emilia.

Chapter Forty

CARTER

I fucking miss her. It's only been a couple of days and USC is even more amazing than I thought it would be, but I fucking miss her. Emilia is so ingrained in my life that everything feels odd without her. I miss her touch and I miss her smile. I miss our conversations and I miss the way my hands wrap around her waist. Hell, I even miss the way she smells.

I'd done so well in drawing a line between us, but my leaving party changed everything all over again. It was obvious that she wanted me just as badly as I wanted her, no matter how hard she tried to convince me otherwise. The look in her eyes when I kissed her and the way she moaned when I sank inside her... she couldn't have been faking that.

I dry my hair with my towel and lean back against the wall. Does she miss me too? We've been texting a lot, but it isn't the same. I toy with my phone and check the time. It's ten pm, so she might be in bed already. I hesitate before pressing the video call icon by her name.

She picks up almost immediately and I grin. Like I thought, she's in bed.

"Hey," she says, her eyes widening. I just got out of the shower and even though I've put on boxer shorts, to her it probably looks like I'm naked. I grin and lie down on my bed. I'm lucky to have a single bed dorm room. Though I would've shared with Asher, it makes calling my Minx easier.

"Hey," I reply. I get comfortable on my bed and Emilia's eyes darken. Even through my small phone screen I can see her looking at me with lust filled eyes, at least that hasn't changed. "See something you like?" I ask. Emilia bites down on her lip and looks away, her cheeks pink.

I cup my neck the way Emilia always likes doing, and her eyes flash heatedly. I run my palm over my chest and down until it's out of view. I'm not actually touching myself, but it's fun to make her think I am.

"So how was your day, Minx?"

She blinks as though she's struggling to focus on what I'm saying, and her response is delayed. It's hot as hell to see her so worked up. She tilts the camera so more of her body is in view and she sits up so the sheets fall away. It's my turn to be shell-shocked now. She's wearing a flimsy silk top that outlines her tits. It's so low that I'd be able to see her nipples if she just moved a bit more. She smiles smugly when she sees my reaction.

"Yeah, it was okay. It's boring without you, to be honest. No one to play pranks on, and Kate has just been sulking. She won't hang out with me either."

I don't think she meant to tell me about Kate, or if she did, she probably assumes I'll believe Kate is sulking because of me. Like that would ever happen.

"Hmm, I never thought my little sister would miss me so much," I say, messing with her. Emilia's eyes widen as though she's only just realized what she said, and she clears her throat awkwardly.

"Uh, yeah. Of course she misses you."

"What about you?" I ask. I'm oddly nervous while I await her answer.

"What about me?" she says, a cute little smile on her face. She knows exactly what I'm asking, but she's being cheeky nonetheless.

"Do you miss me, Minx?"

She runs a hand through her hair, her expression morphing into sadness and loneliness. The look in her eyes mirrors how I feel exactly.

"Yes, Carter. I miss you. I miss you so much more than I thought I would. I miss seeing you every morning and I miss catching glimpses of you from my room. I miss our conversations and I... I miss your hugs," she whispers, her voice breaking.

I inhale deeply. My heart aches. I'm so unhappy without her — I can barely get through my day without finding something I have to tell her about.

"I miss you too, baby," I murmur. "Shit, I think about you all day. I wonder what you're doing and if you're thinking of me. I keep imagining what it'll be like when you finally join me here. By then I'm sure I'll know all there is to know about LA. I'll be able to show you around and I could walk you to your classes. I can't believe I'll have to wait two more years to share this with you."

Emilia sighs, her eyes filled with sorrow. "I can't wait," she whispers. "I'm working as hard as I can to make sure I get a full ride. Thanks to your dad's endless speeches, USC is *my* first choice too. I really hope I'll be able to join you in two years."

I look away, hesitating. "Emilia," I whisper. She looks at me and tilts her head in question. "I don't know. I miss you, baby. I miss you so much. I hate the thought of being so far away and not even being able to call you mine. We can keep it from Kate if you want, but *please*, please tell me you'll be my girlfriend."

She looks at me with wide eyes and I see the flash of excitement in her eyes. I know she wants to say yes, but then rationality overtakes her. She shakes her head even as her eyes are filling with tears.

"Carter, I can't. We can't. Kate has been so vocal about her ending our friendship if I ever dated you. I can't do it knowing that I'll lose her. She's my best friend, Carter. I can't do this, no matter how much I might want to. And you know your mom doesn't approve. She's never asked anything of us before. I don't think I could live with myself if I went behind her back like that. Could you? I think it'll just destroy our relationship in the end."

I feel my anger rise, fueled by my helplessness. "So, you'd rather lose me? Make no mistake, Emilia, things can't stay the way they are now. I'm not going to pine after you, knowing that you can't even put me first. I need you to trust that Kate and Mom will get over it. They'll be mad as hell for a while, but in the end, they'll just want you to be happy."

Emilia shakes her head, a single tear dropping down her cheek. "No, they won't. They won't get over it, Carter. Kate especially will never forgive me."

I sigh and throw my arm over my face to hide my despair. "Minx... I can't do this. I can't go back and forth with you like this. I can't keep waiting for you to finally realize how good we could be together. I can't keep waiting for you to finally put me first."

She looks at me speechlessly. "What does that mean?" she asks, her voice trembling.

I look away, unsure. "I don't know, Minx. I guess it just means we move on. If you don't want us to be together, then I guess we won't be. I don't want to, but I can't keep begging you to be with me. You've made it clear where we stand and you've made your choice. I'll respect that, Emilia, I'll move on. I'll forget we ever even happened, and with time I'm sure things can go back to what they used to be. That's what you want, right?"

I'm praying that she'll say no, that she'll say that this isn't what she wants. That she's changed her mind, and that she wants to be with me after all. But she doesn't. She'd rather lose me than risk upsetting my family. I wish I could hate her for it, but I can't. It's my own family she's putting first.

Emilia nods, and whatever was left of my heart shatters. "Yes, okay. Let's do that," she says.

I nod. That's it — we're done. Now I just have to make myself believe it.

Chapter Forty-One

EMILIA

I'm anxious, and I hate that I am. I've barely heard from Carter in two weeks. If not for the things Kate mentioned, I wouldn't even know if he settled in well or not. I type and retype a text over and over again.

Emilia: *Hey, how are things going?*

I wait for a reply anxiously. He doesn't text back until an hour later. I can't focus on class at all because all I do is glance at my phone.

Devil: *Yeah, good. How are things at home?*

I bite down on my lip and stare at my phone. He's asking how things are at home, he's not asking how I am. I don't really know how to keep a conversation going with Carter these days. It was so effortless when he first moved away. We'd text all the time, and he'd video call me before bed every day.

Ever since that conversation we had about calling things off, he's been distant. He's kept his word, and he's moving on. Part of me actually thought we'd stay close and that we'd still text all the time, but it's quite the opposite. He barely texts and hasn't called me once. I know I'm not his girlfriend, and I know I chose not to be, so I don't have the right to complain about it, but still.

I'm filled with regret. Should I have said yes when he asked me to be his girlfriend? Would I be able to deal with the fallout that would definitely follow between Kate and me? Would I be able to live with the knowledge that I did the one thing Helen asked me not to?

Emilia: *Yeah, things are good! :) Send me some photos of your dorm! I heard you decorated it a bit?*

Carter doesn't reply again for another hour. I don't get it — does he send one text and then immediately put his phone away? He always used to reply to me within seconds. I can't help but overthink things. Eventually he texts me back.

Devil: *Sorry, I'm so swamped with training and practice. My new coach is a lunatic. I barely have time to sleep between football and classes. I'll send you some pics later.*

Emilia: *Okay, don't overwork yourself! Speak to you later :)*

I groan and drop my head to my desk. This is stupid. All my conversations with Carter are short and awkward. It's usually me who's reaching out, too. He warned me he'd move on and I thought I'd be okay with it, but I'm really not.

I sigh and start scrolling through my social media feed. I pause on a photo and stare at it with wide eyes, my heart sinking. Carter was tagged in a photo by some girl. His arms are wrapped around her and they're clearly out somewhere since both of them have drinks in their hands. She's smiling up at him and he's grinning at the camera.

All those evenings I spent waiting for a call or a text, and he's just been going out drinking and hanging out with other girls. I guess I only have myself to blame — he asked me to make things official, and I didn't want to. He's not mine. He's not my boyfriend, and he doesn't owe me anything, but it still hurts like hell.

I throw my phone in my bag when the bell rings. I feel stupid. I'm being stupid. Kate is already seated in the canteen and looks like she hasn't slept in days. I guess Asher being gone is harder on her than she's admitting.

"Hey," she mutters listlessly.

"Hey, what's up? You look like a zombie."

She rolls her eyes and glares at me. "I just really miss Asher," she says. "We said we'd stay friends and things have been going well. I speak to him all the time, but it isn't the same. Asher and Carter have been going out almost every night with their new football team, and I hate it."

I nod in understanding and take a bite of my food, barely tasting it. All I can think about is the photo I saw earlier. He seemed so close to that girl and the way she was looking at him... I can't help but overthink it. When he said he'd move on, I naively thought he meant he'd forget about his feeling and we'd go back to being friends. I didn't think he'd actually get with anyone else. He hasn't so much as looked at anyone in as long as I can remember. The only time I've ever seen him do that was with Gemma, and I'm pretty sure he did that to make me jealous. This time, it doesn't look like that's his aim. It looks like he's truly moving on, and there's nothing I can do about it.

"Hey, you're Emilia, right?"

I look up to find a guy I've never seen before standing in front of our table. I nod and he scratches his nose awkwardly.

"I'm Landon," he says. I nod again. Landon shifts his weight from one foot to the other. "I just wanted to introduce myself. I moved here a few months ago. I noticed you on my first day here and I just haven't been able to get you out of my mind. So, I finally worked up the courage to talk to you, but I don't really know what to say. And I guess maybe... Do you think that maybe you could give me your number?"

I blink up at him. He's rambling like crazy, but rather than being annoying, it's kind of cute. My first instinct is to say no. Though Carter and I aren't together, it still kind of feels like we are. But then I think back to how short he's been with me recently and the photo I saw earlier today. He's moving on, and I need to do the same. If I don't, I'll end up pining after him while he's getting with one girl after the other at college.

I nod at Landon. "Yeah, I guess I could give you my number."

Landon grins at me and fumbles around with his phone before finally handing it over. I type in my number and give myself a missed call before handing it back to him. He grins and puts his phone away. He's surprisingly cute. He's not hot like Carter is, but he's good looking and a little dorky.

"I... uh, I will text you," he says. He turns around and walks away, but he pauses two steps away from me and turns back. "Bye, Emilia," he says. He turns around again and walks off in a rush.

Kate bursts out laughing. "That's one thing I forgot about. With Carter gone, you might actually be able to date. Dude, you might not have to go to college still a virgin," she says, elbowing me. I blush and shake my head. I feel bad for not telling her anything. She's told me about every step she's taken with Asher, but I've kept my own experiences a secret.

"Maybe," I reply. I don't really want to date. I just want Carter.

Chapter Forty-Two

CARTER

I'm excited as I walk into the house. It's been months since I've been back and I've missed the hell out of everyone. I'm excited to be spending Christmas at home. Asher helps me carry my luggage in carefully, and I know he's already looking for Kate. I don't need his help, but he insisted, as though it's not obvious that he can't wait a single second longer to see my sister again. I thought he'd get over her at college for sure, but he hasn't. I haven't seen him look at a single girl in months. It's like he doesn't even register them. I haven't been much better, to be honest. Every time I got close to sleeping with someone, I ended up backing out. My Minx ruined me for everyone else. I'm excited to see her, and I'm excited to see what kind of shit she'll get up to this time. I'm sure she's been planning some absolute mayhem for me.

I walk into my bedroom and stare out the window, straight into hers. I expected to find her studying at her desk, or maybe not even there at all. What I find instead is her in some other guy's arms. She's standing in the middle of her bedroom, her lips against his. The way she's kissing him is passionate and eager. It's obvious that she's learned a thing or two since I kissed her for the first time all those months ago. My heart feels like it's been ripped right out of my chest.

"Carter?" my mom says. She puts her hand on my shoulder and I drag my eyes away from the show Emilia is unknowingly giving me. My mom glances out my window and looks at me with wide eyes before pulling my curtains shut. She looks awkward and then glances away before clearing her throat.

"How long has that been going on?" I ask, my voice low. Even I hear the barely restrained anger in my tone.

My mother looks at me apologetically, and I already know I'm not going to like the answer. "I think they've been together for two months or so?"

I stare down at my shoes. "I've only been at college for less than five months," I say, more to myself than to her. It's no wonder she said she didn't want to do long-distance. Was she ever even serious about me at all? It sure didn't take her long to start dating. I guess with me out of the way, she finally got what she wanted. I still remember how distraught she was when I crashed her date with Tony. I want to be happy for her, but I can't. My heart feels fucking shattered. Maybe she was never really that concerned about Kate. Maybe it's me she didn't want.

"Come on, darling," my mom says. "I made your favorite carrot cake."

I follow her down the stairs and try my best to smile. I don't want her to find out that Emilia has hurt me. I don't want Emilia to know either. She and I were never together, she made sure of it. It's better this way.

My mom fills me in on all the things I've missed, and it's like I never even left. Just like usual, Emilia walks through the door around dinnertime, but this time she has a familiar-looking boy in tow. I think he was in her grade. At least this one isn't scrawny as fuck. He's got nothing on me, but at least he looks better than fucking Tony.

Emilia freezes when she sees me standing in the kitchen, her eyes going wide. She looks so fucking beautiful. How the hell is she more beautiful than in my memories?

"Carter," she says. It takes her a couple of seconds, but then she walks up to me and hugs me. Her familiar smell assaults me and her body still fits against mine perfectly. I stand there, frozen. I don't even hug her back. She pulls away quickly and looks at me, confused.

"Ah, Carter... this is Landon," she says awkwardly. He steps up to me with a wide smile.

"Wow, Carter Clarke. We've never met before, but I've always looked up to you. You were a legend on the field, man. You still playing? I mean, yeah, of course you are."

I nod at him and then glance back at Emilia, but she's avoiding my gaze.

"How do you and Emilia know each other?" I ask, needing to hear it for myself. I see a flicker of panic in her eyes before she looks back down.

Landon throws his arm around Emilia and grins at me. "Oh, well, Emilia and I are dating."

"I see," I murmur. "Well... welcome to the family, London."

He blinks. "Um, it's Landon."

I walk away and plop down on my sofa, wishing I was back at college. I'm so irrationally angry. Emilia and I never promised each other anything so I shouldn't be upset, but damn, I am. Fuck. It's not like I've been a saint while at USC. I told her I'd move on, and I've tried my best to do that. I've gone to parties and I've made out with girls, but I haven't taken anyone on a fucking date. I haven't given anyone my time or my attention, and I haven't even slept with anyone. Meanwhile, Emilia has been dating someone else. She wouldn't be my girlfriend, but she's happy to be someone else's. My fucked up mind can't help but wonder if he knows her body better than I do. If she's done things with him she's never done with me. If she's been on dates with him I'll never get to take her on.

Him being here means she's obviously introduced him to my

parents and her dad, so it's serious enough. What the fuck was she thinking bringing him into my house while I'm here? Did she ever care for me at all? How could she possibly think this wouldn't hurt me?

Emilia approaches and sits down next to me, her thighs grazing mine. I glare at her and she shrinks back.

"Landon?" I ask.

She bites down on her lip and looks away as though she can't face me. I sigh and shake my head.

"I didn't know you'd be back today," she says, as though that makes anything even remotely better. Would she have kept this from me if I hadn't found out today? I wanted to surprise my family and her by showing up a few days earlier than planned. Who would've known I'd be the one ending up surprised?

"I hope you're happy, Minx," I mutter before walking away from her and straight out the door.

Chapter Forty-Three

EMILIA

Carter has been acting weird all week. We've barely spoken in the last couple of months, but I thought things would mostly go back to normal once he was back here. Instead, he's just been avoiding me. It's like I don't even exist. I should've told him about Landon, but it never came up. All our conversations are a variation of 'hey how're you doing, I'm fine and you?'

Meanwhile, he kept being tagged in photos with girls, though in most of them he's with the same blonde. I've purposely avoided asking him who she is because I have a feeling I might not like the answer. One of the main reasons I started dating Landon is because of those photos, because of all the evidence that he's moving on. That still doesn't mean I'd ever want to confront him with Landon though.

I don't know what to do to make things better between us. I don't want us to be estranged — I want to at least be friends with Carter. I rummage through my wardrobe and take out my prank box. Eventually, I find what I'm looking for and grin. No matter how bad our arguments get, a good prank usually fixes things. I'm hoping that'll be the case now too.

I sneak into his bedroom with a handful of fake cockroaches. I know he hates them, but I have some fond memories of the last time I pulled this trick. I can hear his shower running and grin. He'll get the shock of his life when he gets into bed later. If I'm lucky, he'll keep his curtains open and I'll get to witness his horror for myself. I place the cockroaches on his bed strategically. He'll feel them before he sees them.

The shower cuts off abruptly and I freeze. The door opens, and I jump behind his curtain to hide. I never would've made it to the door. I stand as still as I can. Usually he takes really long showers, so why the hell is he already out of there?

I peek at him from behind the curtain and bite down on my lip when I spot him. He's wearing nothing but a towel that's hanging low on his hips. Just one tug would have the whole thing unravelling. I'm instantly wet and needy. His body looks even better than it did when he left. I guess he wasn't lying about the training being tough. He's all muscle. His pecs and his abs look good enough to lick, and I regret never having done that before.

Carter drops the towel and a small gasp escapes my lips. He freezes and I hide, standing dead still. Eventually I hear his footsteps moving away and I take another peek. Damn, his ass is fucking magnificent. I blush and take my time admiring his body.

I'll need to find a way to get out of here. Carter has been in a weird mood lately and I'm dead if he catches me now. He'll make me freaking eat the cockroaches. I pat myself down and close my eyes in despair. I left my damn phone in the living room, so Kate can't even come to the rescue.

Carter walks back towards me and my heart hammers in my chest. He pulls the curtains aside, exposing me. I stare at him with wide eyes and a guilty expression on my face. He looks at me intensely, his expression wavering between lust and anger. It's not often that I can't read him, but tonight I truly don't know what he's thinking.

My eyes involuntarily wander down his body, and I bite down on my lip. He's put on boxer shorts, but nothing else. He's hard and his boxers aren't hiding it well at all. He sees me staring and places a finger underneath my chin to lift my gaze back up.

"My eyes are up here, Minx," he says, his voice low and dangerous. I'm breathing hard and barely manage to hold his gaze.

"What are you doing here, Emilia?"

I hesitate and glance at his bed. His eyes follow my gaze and he chuckles.

"Hmm, here for a sleepover maybe? I wonder what your little boyfriend will think of that..."

I blink, startled. Landon. How the hell did I completely forget about Landon? I look away. Ever since Carter came back, he's been all I can think about. I've barely even spoken to Landon in days now.

"What kind of mischief did you get up to, huh? We're not kids anymore, Emilia. Enough with this now."

I stare at him, speechless. *Enough?* Pulling pranks on each other has always been our thing. I can't imagine a world in which we didn't do that. Carter closes the distance between us and my hands find their way around his neck. They move entirely of their own volition.

I feel something poking me in my stomach, but I don't dare look down. He's hard. It feels like a steel pipe is pushed up against me, and I instantly remember what it's like to have him inside me. Landon and I haven't done much more than make out. He's been pushing for more and his hands have started to wander, but I'm not ready — I'm not comfortable enough with him. Having Carter this close to me feels entirely different though. My entire body tenses with anticipation. I'm trembling and getting wet just from having him close.

"Tell me, Minx. Why did you sneak into my room? Looking for something your boyfriend can't give you?"

Carter pushes his hips against me and my lips fall open. He

grins when I fail to hide the lust I'm feeling. His forehead drops to mine and his hands wrap around my waist. He pulls me into him roughly, my breasts crashing against his chest.

I automatically arch my back, my eyes dropping to his lips. Carter grins, but there's no amusement in his eyes. His eyes trail down my body and he hooks my leg up. I automatically wrap it around his hip. My skirt rides up and he runs a finger over my soaking wet panties.

"Hmm, you're still getting so wet for me, Minx. Tell me, do you get this wet for Landon? Does he fuck you the way I do? Has he had you in your bed? In our treehouse?"

His finger slips past my underwear and into me. I moan when he rubs against my clit and my entire body trembles with need. I'm seconds away from coming already. It's been too long. This is exactly why things never went any further with Landon, because I don't feel the same desperation to be with him.

Carter chuckles and pushes me further and further until I'm about to burst. Right before I come, he pulls away, leaving me hanging. I whimper and look up at him pleadingly, but his expression hardens.

"No more petty little games, Minx. We're done. We're not children anymore, Emilia. Enough now. You're dating someone. How would Landon feel if he knew you were sneaking into my bedroom at night? How would he feel if he saw us right now?"

I gulp. I know he's right, but I don't know if I could stop if I tried. Messing with Carter comes so naturally to me... it's the way we communicate. If he were to stop, it'd feel like he stopped caring about me.

"You're my little sister's best friend, Emilia. I'm merely your neighbor and perhaps a family friend. Let's start acting like it."

Carter pulls away and walks to his bedroom door. He holds it open for me and closes it as soon as I walk out.

Chapter Forty-Four

CARTER

I feel like a fucking fool. I wish I'd never come back for Christmas. Just seeing Emilia fucking hurts. Thankfully, I haven't had to see her with Landon since that first day, but just knowing she is someone else's tears me apart.

She clearly didn't give a shit about me if it only took her three months to get over me and start dating someone else. I practically begged her to be my girlfriend *twice*, and I pursued her for an entire year. Yet she starts dating Landon within three months. It's obvious I've been an idiot. I thought she was genuinely worried about her friendship with Kate, but now I'm wondering if that might have been an excuse. Maybe she didn't know how to tell me she didn't have feelings for me. Maybe to her, I was nothing more than a friend with benefits, while I thought she was the love of my life.

Emilia walks into the house and freezes when she sees me. Things are so awkward between us now. Maybe she was right all along. She and I never should've gotten together. Rather than joining Kate and me on the sofa like she usually would've done, she disappears into the kitchen instead.

"She's been weird since you got back," Kate tells me. She glances at me suspiciously and I look away.

"We just kind of grew apart while I was gone. I haven't really spoken to her in months now." Just admitting that much hurts, but it's true. We said we'd move on, and we have. I'm not sure how long it'll take us to get back to normal. I'm not sure we ever will.

Kate nods, and it annoys me that she looks somewhat pleased. "I actually kind of thought she had a thing for you, you know. I'm glad she doesn't. Can you imagine how messed up things would get if you two dated and broke up?"

If only she knew the half of it. "Why did you think she had a thing for me?" I ask, unable to curb my curiosity.

Kate looks at me in disbelief. "Dude, are you blind? The way she used to look at you sometimes was just straight up indecent. It was so awkward. I was terrified she'd seduce you or something, like all my other friends. I love you both too much to let that happen. You'd be a disaster together."

Her words grate on me. I can't understand why she hates the idea of us so much. "Unlike her and London?"

She rolls her eyes. "It's Landon. *Landon*, and yeah. They're so cute together. He freaking adores her. I feel like she only sorta liked you because no one else ever had a chance to approach her. You were kind of her only choice. And the way you two argue and mess with each other is insane. I can't even imagine how awful you two would be together if you ever dated. God, can you imagine just how devastated Mom would be if you broke up and Emilia stopped coming over? We both know Emilia is secretly her favorite child. And, you know, forget about you breaking up — just your arguments would affect everyone so much. I'd hate it, and I know Mom would too."

I don't even know what to say to that, not that it matters at this point. "Either way, she and I are just friends, if that. I wouldn't worry about it."

Kate nods and sighs in relief. "Thank God for that. I'm so relieved she's dating Landon now. You two were just a disaster in the making."

I nod, trying my best to ignore the dull ache in my chest. Is it true? Did Emilia only want me because she didn't have anyone else to choose from? Is it because I kept everyone else away from her? I'm not too sure. I didn't treat her that much differently to how I treated Kate, and Kate still managed to go on a bunch of dates, some of which I'm sure were with my own best friend.

Emilia walks into the living room and smiles at me tightly before sitting next to Kate. She's wearing a short dress that rides up when she sits down, and I'm instantly reminded of the way I pinned her against my window a few days ago. I was furious and I wanted her so badly. I shouldn't have touched her the way I did, but hell, she shouldn't have responded the way she did. She was soaking wet. Three more seconds and she'd have come all over my fingers.

"Okay, so, The Grinch or Home Alone?" Kate asks. Emilia grins and I know this is going to take forever, because she loves both of them wholeheartedly. The way she smiles makes my heart feel funny. When did I even fall for her? I can't pinpoint a moment from after which I thought of her as mine. I think I might very well always have been in love with Emilia Parker.

I sigh and walk away. There's no way I can get through an evening of watching movies with her, pretending nothing is wrong, when not a single thing in my world feels right. I walk into my bedroom and stare outside. How many times have we exchanged messages through our windows? How many times have I sat here watching her instead of doing my homework?

The door behind me opens and Emilia walks in, quickly closing it behind her. She pauses and leans against the door.

"Hey," she says.

"Hey."

Emilia has never been awkward or polite with me, not even once. It's weird that we're acting like we're strangers.

"Can we talk?" she asks. I nod and she walks to my bed. She sits down and clearly expects me to come sit down next to her, but I walk towards my desk chair instead.

"You've been weird," Emilia says. I look at her, unsure how to even reply to that.

"Weird how?"

She shrugs, as though she can't quite pinpoint it either.

"I asked you to be my girlfriend, and you said no. We both moved on. You moved on quicker than I did, but whatever. We're back to what we used to be, aren't we? Just friends, or something like that."

Emilia shakes her head. "But we're not, Carter. We aren't friends. You're just avoiding me and you won't speak to me. Even pranks are off the table now," she says, her voice breaking.

I sigh and run a hand through my hair. "I don't know what you want from me, Emilia. When I offered you the world, it was too much. Now that I'm treating you the way you asked me to, it isn't enough. Nothing will ever please you, and I'm done trying. Let's just treat each other civilly in front of our families and let's just let things be. Maybe we'll find a way to go back to what we were before, maybe we won't."

She gulps and looks at me, tears gathering in her eyes. I look away. I can't stand to see the pain in her expression, but I know I need a clean break.

"That would be okay with you?" she asks, her voice faltering. "If you and I were nothing more than strangers, would that be okay with you?"

No. It wouldn't be. But it'll have to be.

"Yes," I say.

Emilia nods and turns to walk out. Every fiber of my being is yelling for me to follow her, but I know I can't. Emilia has made her choice, and it's time I accept that. She and I will never be together, and I need to learn to be okay with that. Not every story has a happy ending, and I guess ours is just one of those.

———————

Read Book II: Illicit Promises

Illicit Promises Chapter 1

Emilia

I'm trembling as Kate and I walk up to the apartment that Carter and Asher share. My hands are clammy and my heart is hammering in my chest.

Carter and I haven't had a single real conversation in the last year and a half. Every time he came home he went out of his way to avoid me. If he was ever forced to speak to me, he'd treat me with such indifference that I'd barely recognize him. Ever since the first time he came home, he and I have slowly but surely become strangers. Carter now treats me with the same cold politeness that he used to reserve for Kate's other friends. It's like *he and I* were never friends. Like we weren't so much more than that. I'm terrified of seeing him again. I'm terrified of him pushing me away even further.

I've been in a weird state of denial, telling myself that we're only distant because he's been so far away, but soon I'll be out of excuses. I'm not sure I'm ready to deal with the guy he's become. Carter and I used to be so close, but now I barely know him. All I know is whatever I hear from Kate and Helen, combined with what I see on social media and on the news. He's a rising football star and based on the photos I've seen online, well loved by the girls at USC. While I logically know he isn't the guy I used to know, my heart refuses to accept it. In the few interviews he's done on his private life, he made it clear that he doesn't believe in love at all and that he greatly enjoys his bachelor lifestyle. The Carter I used to know wasn't like that. He might never have said it, but I'm pretty sure he used to love me as much as I loved him.

The door opens, and Asher appears, his eyes lingering on Kate. I know the two of them have been seeing each other on and off again — neither one of them able to stay away, though they both keep trying. All the while they've done their best to keep it from Carter, promising each other to keep it quiet until they finally decide to make things official, which has yet to happen. For Kate, Carter's graduation party was the start of something new. It was the night she and Asher finally gave in and acted on their feelings, setting in motion the months of push and pull they've gone through. For me, it was the end of the best thing I ever had. The night I spent with Carter was the last night we had together.

Asher pulls Kate towards him and hugs her tightly, his face buried in her hair. When they're still wrapped up in each other minutes later, I clear my throat awkwardly. Asher blinks and looks at me, confused. Yep. He didn't even see me standing here. He blushes and steps back to let us in.

"Hey, Emilia," he murmurs. I roll my eyes and push past him. If they're going to be this obvious about their affection for each other, then they might as well not even try to keep it from Carter. They're hardly very subtle. For just a split second, I wonder what things might have been like if Carter and I started dating two years ago. Would we have made it? Would Helen and Kate have gotten over it? Would he be welcoming me the way Asher is welcoming Kate? My heart aches at the mere thought of all the would-haves and could-haves.

"Make yourself at home," Asher tells us. Kate and I follow him in curiously. The apartment looks so normal. It doesn't at all look like the bachelor pad I was expecting. It's just a regular two-bedroom apartment with mostly neutral colored furniture. It isn't even remotely messy. The boys can do with a bit of color, but they certainly haven't done a bad job.

We pause in front of Carter's bedroom and Kate sighs. "Is he still asleep?" she asks, her mood souring. I check my watch and bite down on my lip. It's nine am on a Sunday, but he knew we'd get here today. I might not have spoken to him much, but I know Kate has.

Kate rolls her eyes and opens his bedroom door. I hesitate before following her in. Will he be happy to see me at all? Will he be upset if we wake him up? Things haven't been the same between us in months now, but I'm hoping we can at least become friends again now that we'll be seeing a lot of each other.

It's pitch dark when we walk in, and Kate slams her hand against the light switch angrily. Carter's room is bathed in light and he groans. My eyes roam over his room in surprise. His floor is scattered with clothes and other mess. Carter was never super tidy, but he was certainly never this messy either.

Carter sits up and runs a hand through his hair, an annoyed expression on his face. The sheets fall to his waist and my eyes fall to his body. It looks like he's naked and the sheets only barely cover him. He looks mad as hell to have been woken up, but his anger drains away once his eyes land on us. He looks at Asher first, and then at Kate.

"Kate," he says, his voice rough and sleepy. His eyes linger on me for just a few seconds, his expression entirely unreadable. I can't figure out if he's even remotely happy to see me. He dismisses me easily and looks back at Kate. "When did you get here?" he asks. He grabs his jeans from the floor and pulls them on underneath the covers before standing up.

My heart aches at how easily he ignores me. He's focused entirely on Kate, and it's like I'm not even here. He hasn't so much as smiled at me.

"A few minutes ago," Kate says. She crosses her arms over each other and glares at him. "I told you Milly and I would get here today. Why are you still in bed?"

I look up at him as discreetly as I can. He looks bigger. More muscular and rugged. I'm hit with a familiar sense of longing. My eyes roam over his body hungrily and my gaze freezes on his lower abdomen. He's got more than a few little kiss marks on his skin and I suddenly feel sick. I bite down on my lip harshly to keep my emotions in check. It feels like someone has stabbed me in the heart and then twisted the knife. It's been over a year since Carter and I ended things, so why do I still feel this way? I look away, frozen in place.

I breathe in as deeply as I can, my breath hitching. It really hurts. He warned me that he'd move on, but I guess I was in denial. Carter has done his best to hide his sex life from Kate and me. I always *knew*, but knowing isn't the same as seeing. I take a step back and rub my chest as though that'll soothe my aching heart.

"I thought Asher told you that our orientation is tomorrow. I literally called you last night to make sure you'd be up in time. I can't believe you're still in bed," she says, snapping at him.

Asher clears his throat and puts his hand on Kate's shoulder. "Come on," he says. "I'll show you my room and the rest of the place while Carter gets ready. It won't take him long."

Kate glares at Carter one more time and then follows Asher. I trail behind them quietly.

"I... uh... I'll make some coffee," I say, tipping my head towards the kitchen. I need a moment to pull myself together. Seeing Carter is so much harder on me than I thought it would be. It's like feelings I thought were long gone came rushing back at once. I guess part of me hoped there'd still be *something* between us. I never got over him, but it seems like he's definitely moved on. I can't help but blame myself. I should've chosen to be with him while I still could.

Kate looks at me worriedly and I smile at her. "Just tired," I tell her, lying through my teeth. She hesitates, but eventually nods and follows Asher.

I walk around the kitchen numbly, working mostly on autopilot. I don't snap out of it until Carter walks in. Looks like he didn't actually bother getting ready — he's still in nothing but his jeans, his chest exposed. Carter leans back against one of the counters and studies me curiously.

I push a cup of coffee towards him wordlessly, a small insincere smile on my face. I've been standing here completely spaced out for so long that the coffee is now lukewarm at best. Usually I'd have offered to make him a new cup, but I just don't have it in me today. My heart feels shattered. Is this what Carter and I have become? Strangers that don't even say hi anymore?

My eyes involuntarily drop down to the kiss marks on his skin, and I'm hit with another flash of pain. Carter looks down and traces the marks with his fingers, a small frown on his face. I look away and stare at my cup instead.

"Hmm, looks like my friends and I had a bit too much fun last night," he says, grinning roguishly.

I feel sick to my stomach and grit my teeth. "You fuck all of your friends?" I ask, my voice harsh and angry. I can't help it. I promised myself I'd be better than this, but I can't help myself.

Carter looks startled and then chuckles. "Emilia, I'm single and I'm a football player. I'm not gonna stand here and pretend like I've been a saint. We're at college, for God's sake. It's not like you've been a saint back home. How's Landon these days?"

I frown. "Landon?" I ask, confused. I haven't even thought about him in a year. "We broke up like a year and a half ago.".

Carter straightens and stares at me with wide eyes. "You *what*?"

I look away and wrap my arms around myself. I broke up with Landon the first time Carter came home from college. I still remember the exact moment that I knew Landon and I would never work out. I tried pulling a prank on Carter and he caught me. Carter had me pressed up against his window, his fingers buried deep inside me. I knew right there and then that I'd never want Landon the same way and that it would be unfair to keep dating him, when I knew I was just using him to get over Carter. I broke up with Landon the very next day.

"I only dated him because I was wondering what dating might be like. It wasn't really as good as I thought it would be, so I ended things."

Carter blinks in disbelief. "Why didn't you tell me?" he asks, his eyes flashing with anger.

I frown and cross my arms over my chest. "When was I supposed to tell you, Carter? Whenever you came home, you ignored me. Besides, why would you even care?"

Carter runs a hand through his hair and looks at me through narrowed eyes. "You said it wasn't that good. *What* wasn't that good? Did you sleep with him?"

I shake my head instinctively and immediately regret it. Carter's lips tug up at the edges and his entire demeanor relaxes. I grit my teeth and glare at him.

"It's none of your business who I have or haven't slept with, you manwhore."

Carter chuckles. "Hmm, okay, Minx," he murmurs. My heart skips a beat and I hide my face in my coffee cup. He hasn't called me *Minx* in months. It's always Emilia these days. To hear him call me the way he used to oddly revives the butterflies that I try so hard to keep buried.

"So those two times with me are the only times you've had sex, huh? You're practically still a virgin, Minx. At this rate you might as well keep it up until marriage."

I almost choke on my coffee and cough violently. Carter grins as though my unease is amusing him. I poke him on the chest angrily. "Whose fault is that, Carter? You kept everyone away from me. Even after you left most guys didn't dare come near me."

I'm shaking with anger. Even though we always denied it, everyone always saw me as Carter's girl; as the girl that's out of reach unless you want to deal with Carter himself. Long after he left, people would ask me how he's doing. Other than Landon, there weren't many guys that could even look at me without immediately associating me with Carter. Not that it would've mattered. No one captured my interest anyway. In the last two years, I couldn't even imagine sleeping with anyone other than Carter. I still can't.

"Seems like you don't have that issue, huh? You're far from virginal, aren't you?" I say angrily, my voice breaking. I'm consumed with pain and rage that I know I have no right to feel. I glance at my coffee cup, longing to give into my temper and dump my coffee on his head dramatically. It won't mend my broken heart, but still.

Carter laughs and tips his head towards my coffee cup. "Do it. I dare you," he murmurs.

I grit my teeth and glare at him. I can't believe he still reads me so well. I hate it. I hate that he still owns every piece of me. "Don't think I won't," I snap.

Carter crosses his arms and grins at me provocatively. I glare at him and rise to my tiptoes, my coffee cup in hand. I bring it to his head slowly and Carter merely looks at me in amusement, as though he's waiting to see whether I'll actually do it. I hold my cup over his head and empty it slowly, looking him in the eye as I do it. Coffee streams all over his face and down his body. He could've evaded me easily, but instead he leans back against the counter as coffee streams down his body.

My eyes follow the trail down his abdomen and a moment that should've felt victorious and vindictive instantly turns into *more*. I lick my lips and try to keep my mind off licking the coffee off his body. I swallow hard and Carter's eyes darken as though he knows exactly what I'm thinking.

The moment shatters when my eyes zero in on the kiss marks on his skin. Just looking at them makes me feel like I've been sucker punched. How many girls know exactly what Carter's abs taste like? Hell... some girl probably still has the taste of him on her lips. I look away, equal parts disgusted and heartbroken. It's obvious he's been spending his days fucking around.

He's clearly moved on, just like he said he would. So why am I still stuck in the past? Why am I unable to even want anyone else? Seems like Carter is having great sex and I'm missing out. I'm missing out because I keep comparing every man I meet to the one I can no longer have. No more. I'm going to live it up at college as much as Carter has. Maybe that's exactly what I need to finally get over him. Seems to have worked fine for him. I'll find someone to sleep with before the week is over. How hard can it really be?

I grit my teeth and Carter grabs my jaw. He turns my face towards his and shakes his head. "It's not happening, Minx. Whatever you have in mind right now, forget about it. It isn't happening."

I glare at him, hating that he can still read me so well. "We'll see about that, Carter."

Keep reading Illicit Promises here

Made in the USA
Las Vegas, NV
05 May 2024

89566796R00132